Murder Gets the Boot

by
Mike Bartosik

PublishAmerica
Baltimore

First printing

ISBN: 1-4137-6038-4
PUBLISHED BY PUBLISHAMERICA, LLLP
www.publishamerica.com
Baltimore

Printed in the United States of America

This book is for Josie
Thanks for your faith in me

To Aunt Dora —
Hope you enjoy the
story.

Mike

Chapter 1

I guess you could say that when it comes to making decisions I'm just about the same as everyone else. The small, day-to-day kinds of choices (what to have for breakfast, whether to take the garbage out before or after the football game, etc.) I make on the fly. Got a choice? Pick one and let's move on with life. So what if I decide to have eggs for breakfast only to discover that there's no bread for toast? I'll change to cereal.

There's a second level of decision, the one that may have a small consequence if I choose wrong, but nothing I can't survive. Buy the wrong kind of car? Okay, an inconvenience, but a couple of years of driving around in a car that looked good in the showroom but turned out to be a piece of junk is no great hardship. This is the kind of decision I, like most people, take a moderate amount of time making, using whatever information I happen to have at hand.

The third type of decisions, the big ones, the life-altering decisions, I make slowly and with great care. I look at all aspects of the situation, weigh all the important, and not-so-important, factors, and then make my choice. I then spend years, like everyone else, second-guessing myself. In this third category are decisions such as whether or not to get married; whether to have kids (no matter what your choice was on getting married); and where to live. I've never been married, nor have I faced that choice. I don't have children, but that's a story all its own. But where to live! Everybody has to live somewhere, call someplace home. I made my decision and now call home Pittsfield, Massachusetts.

Pittsfield is in Berkshire County (and is, by the way, the county seat), on the far western side of the state. The Berkshires have long been the summer home of the rich and lazy cream of American society. You can still see the "summer cottages" of nineteenth-century millionaires. I say cottages because that's what they called them. I call them the biggest damn houses I have ever seen. Some are currently serving as resort hotels, nestled coyly among the rolling hills between Pittsfield and Lenox. Over the past twenty years or so the Berkshires, while continuing to serve as the summer getaway for the very rich and very lazy, has opened its doors to include the very obnoxious cream of what today passes for American society. As a matter of fact, within the last five years the Berkshires has come to rival Cape Cod and the Eastern Shore as the hot vacation spot in Massachusetts. Should we ever overtake Cape Cod and become number one, we can look forward to being the summer home of the disgustingly rich, disgustingly lazy and "Don't bother talking to me, just clean my car" cream of American society. Needless to say, I look forward to that day; it's been awhile since I last told somebody to go to hell!

But for over three hundred years the Berkshires has also been the home of year-round, hard-working, and somewhat insular people of good New England stock. And nowhere typifies this like Pittsfield! There is a certain closeness to the community. Okay, maybe "closeness" isn't quite the right word; incestuous might better describe it. By no means am I talking about the six-toes-on-the-left-foot brand of incest. I mean the kind of relationships where when you go to a wedding, the bride's second cousin's father-in-law is your boss. You can't meet anybody new in this town without them knowing somebody you know or are related to. The six degrees of familiarity are reduced by at least five parameters in Pittsfield. In my case, that situation is lessened somewhat by the fact that since I moved to Pittsfield from somewhere else, I'm not related to anyone here (if what I said earlier about not having any children is still true). But I do know a load of people. In my old job, it was impossible not meet people, usually by arresting them. I used to be a cop.

But that brings me back to my discourse on making big decisions. Why Pittsfield? Was there something magical about the city? Was there a golden opportunity staring me in the face in this oasis in the mountains? Am I stupid? Depending on who you ask, the answers to these questions, in order, are no, no, and possibly.

About thirteen years ago I was in the process of being discharged from the service. Since my father, who was an executive with a large multinational corporation, had moved our family from city to city as I was growing up, I had no place to call home. One of my friends in the service just happened to be from Pittsfield. He regaled me with stories of the great winter skiing, the beautiful forests to hike in during the fall and spring, the glimmering mountain lakes to frolic in during the pleasantly warm summers. So I came. That's it! That's how I made this big, life-altering decision: I just listened to my friend's advice and did not even bother to investigate any of the alternatives. After thirteen years, the jury is still out on whether I made the right choice. For some reason I can't fathom, that man is still my friend. I thought I should mention all of this in order to explain why I was being stopped by the police on my way to a murder investigation in the city of Pittsfield.

The spinning red light in my rear-view mirror wasn't unexpected. It's not that I knew I was speeding—I wasn't. Nor was it because I had seen the police cruiser hiding behind the bush inside the chain link fence at the playground—I had. No, the reason I knew the light would be there was because it was always there when I was on my way to work. And I wasn't overly upset about being stopped again. I recognized the cop. He wasn't a friend, more an acquaintance. I had met him right after he had joined the force and just before I left it. As I pulled my car over to the curb, shifted into park and rolled down the window of my car, I smiled. This was going to be a social call.

The crisp air of a Berkshire spring day hit my face, doing a better job of waking me from my thoughts than the coffee sitting in the car's cup holder had done. Spring in the Berkshires, brief as it may be, is great for shaking off winter's lingering cobwebs. Most mornings this time of year start off almost as cold as January, thanks to the saturated ground and the lack of anything really green sprouting up. But come noon, with the sun as high in the sky as it was going to get, the air warms up, the puddles lose their thin layer of ice and are able to slowly evaporate to become the later spring rain. That's what happens "most mornings." Unfortunately, the last couple of days had been out of the ordinary. No, not frigid reminders of winter, but teasing signs of the summer to come. The only thing typical about Berkshire weather is that it is never typical.

"How ya doin', Lieutenant?" beamed Sammy Brackens as he approached my car, his almost-cherubic face somehow out of synch with the dark blue patrolman's uniform he wore. *I used to be that young once*, I thought, *in another lifetime.*

"Doing just fine, Sammy," I answered, sticking my head forward through the open window. "And it's 'Barry,' not 'Lieutenant.' I've been off duty four years now."

"Whatever you say," laughed the cop. "Saw you shoot by me back at Onota Street, thought I'd say hello."

"I appreciate that, Sammy." I grinned back. I had a hunch that wasn't quite the truth. It probably would have been more accurate to say: "I've been waiting for you" at Onota Street.

Whenever I get called in on a job the entire Pittsfield Police Department goes on alert. They know they won't get any information from the suits inside the force when it comes to the big cases, so they have to do an end run and get it from me. I had heard that they have the situation down to a science. When the call goes out informing the "blues" that I'm on a case, sentries are sent to key points around the city in hopes of spotting me. Usually the sentries, like Sammy, are low men on the seniority totem pole. But they get to be big men for a day if they grab me and find out the dope. And there was going to be quite a bit of dope on this one; it was a murder case. Unfortunately,

Sammy spotted me on the way to the crime scene, so even I didn't have any dope yet.

"So what's new, Lieutenant?"

"Nothing much. Just on my way to Cyber. Something big seems to be happening there, although I'm not sure what." I didn't consider that a lie, just part of the cat-and-mouse game.

"Yeah," continued the young cop. "I heard something over the radio about Cyber." A short hesitation on his part, then: "I thought they mentioned something about...a murder."

"I thought I heard that word, too, from Johnston when he called me this morning," I agreed.

It was obvious Sammy was getting a little antsy from playing the game a bit longer than he had anticipated. He shuffled his feet, took a slow, long look down West Street, then back at me.

"Well, just wanted to say hello," he finally said.

I was feeling sorry for the kid, but there really wasn't anything I could do at this point; I just didn't have any information yet. So I threw him a bone. "You still hanging out at Jake's Place?" I asked.

"Yeah, about two or three times a week after work."

"You know, I don't think I've been there for a couple of months now," I lied. I go there just about every day. "Think maybe I'll drop in tonight. See some of the gang."

Sammy's face lit up. He could pump me for information to his heart's delight later when I had something to give. Besides, there was at least two free drinks in the offing now.

"Maybe I'll see you there, Lieutenant. I'm off at five o'clock."

"What a coincidence," I said smiling. "That's about the time I usually get thirsty. See you later, Sammy." I watched the young cop walk back to his car, his gait a little faster and lighter than a policeman's walk should be. It was obvious I was going to hold court later that afternoon.

I started the car and pulled out into the morning commute. Traffic was usually heavy on West Street in the early morning, and today was no exception. Working on the east side of town was fine; living on the west side was even better. Cyber Inc., the largest employer in the city, had its offices and plants spread amidst the rolling hills of an industrial park on East Street. Why did it have rolling green hills instead of acres of asphalt? Why, to hide the polluted groundfill left over from an earlier industrial complex of course. The people of western Massachusetts are nothing if not ecologically aware. At least half of Cyber's employees must have lived on the west side, and at least half of those must take West Street into work. I joined the crowd.

I kept the window rolled down. The spring breeze felt good after the usual long winter. It was early April and the weather had decided to act up once again. It had been 80 degrees the past two days, with the weathermen promising another three days of the same. April in the Berkshire's was never meant for that kind of heat. Buds were popping up on all the trees, and I knew they were going to be sorry. We had the same kind of weather last year in April, followed by a snowstorm in May that dropped 13 inches of the white stuff on everything. Most of the apple crop, one of the largest industries in western Massachusetts, bit the dust. It was going to happen again. But then I don't particularly care for apples, so for now I was going to enjoy the warmth of the sun on my face and the fresh scent of the Berkshire Mountains in my nostrils.

I have told myself many times that on the day I die I want it to be on a beautiful spring morning just like this; I want the fragrances and the feel of the sun to be the last thing I remember of life. So I decided to go to Cyber Inc. by way of Park Square. First of all, Park Square is a circle, a rotary circle. For years it was the only rotary circle in the world where cars already in the circle had to yield to cars entering. That would not necessarily make for a dangerous situation if the only people who drove in Pittsfield were from town and knew that little secret. Unfortunately, we get a lot of tourists and they seem to be used to a different set of driving rules. So after a few decades of horrendous accidents and near-death experiences by the bagful, city officials gave in to the whiners and changed the circle so it followed the same traffic rules as everywhere else in the world. Only the word hasn't quite gotten out to everyone yet. So people in the circle think, and rightly so, that they have the right of way; and people just entering the circle think they have the right of way, just like old times; and the private ambulance companies laugh all the way to the bank (after a short stop at the hospital to drop off their cargo).

As it happened, however, my death wish went unfulfilled for the moment and I safely negotiated the circle, albeit with a dirty look and an obscene gesture from an old lady in a car the size of my house. I continued down East Street and in about five minutes was at the main gate of Cyber Inc. I recognized the guard from earlier visits but had never bothered to learn his name. That pleasure was going to have wait once again, as Mikah Johnston, CEO of Cyber, had let me know in our earlier phone conversation that I should move certain parts of my anatomy quickly in getting to the main plant where the offices were located. The guard must have been given a similar message regarding his anatomy because he merely waved me on with a curt nod.

A few minutes later I was winding my way through the hallways of Cyber Inc.'s executive offices, heading for Mikah Johnston's office. Johnston, as I said, was the CEO of Cyber Inc. and my sometime boss. I say "sometime" because I was on retainer to the company, not a fulltime employee. Why should I be? I was a private investigator, and how many times in one year would a company need an investigator? Only when someone was stealing more than pens and paper clips from the company, or for the extremely sensitive background checks on important employees, or for times when there was a dead body in the building, like now.

"Pete, make sure you get pictures from every angle," boomed a voice I recognized at once. I smiled, not because I liked the man behind the voice, but because I didn't. And he didn't like me. I smiled because I knew my presence would aggravate him. Hey, it's the small things in life that give us the greatest pleasure.

I continued up the hallway and made a left turn at its end. Immediately in front of me was the ubiquitous yellow police tape crossing a doorway. I took a few steps forward and looked in the room that was being cordoned off. It contained a row of vending machines along the wall to my right, two medium-sized folding tables

11

in the middle of the room and a small microwave and coffee maker on a counter that ran along the back wall. I was obviously looking in the employee break room.

The room was also filled with people I recognized. Everyone was busy with some task. One was writing in a notebook; another was photographing the room; a third was rummaging through the pockets of his coat, looking for who-knows what. A fourth was simply standing in the middle of the room, his back to me, directing the other three men. There was still another man in the room, but I didn't recognize him. Not because I had never seen him before, maybe I had. But I couldn't tell from where I stood and where he lay. He was face down on the floor, a pool of drying blood arching outward from his head. The man who was searching his pockets looked up and saw me. He smiled.

"Hi, Barry," he beamed. It was Fred Martin, my first partner on the force and still one of my best friends.

"Hello, Fred. Thought I'd see you here."

I don't know whether it was the mention of my name by Fred or the sound of my voice, but I saw the man whose back was to me shake a little. He turned towards me.

"Dunleavy!" boomed Police Chief Dave Sarcovich, "booming" being the only tone of voice I had ever heard him use. "Get the hell out of here! This is a police scene."

I smiled. "I always thought what was inside the yellow tape was the official crime scene, Chief. And by the looks of it, I'm outside the tape."

Fred, Pete Jacobs, the cop who had been taking photographs, and the third police officer in the room, Donny Prouett, all smiled slightly. They knew that remark was not going to make the Chief happy. They also knew that was why I had said it. Sarcovich, who was taller than me by a good three inches and heavier by at least seventy pounds, stalked towards me, his face quickly changing to various shades of red as he came forward.

"Don't give me any of your wise crap," he said as he walked. "I told you to get out and I mean it. This is a murder investigation and I don't want any interference from you." He was up to the doorway now, glaring down at me. His face and neck were as crimson as I had ever seen them, both his fists clenched, only the thin yellow tape separating us. His head was shaking slightly and I knew he wanted to land one of his giant fists squarely on my nose. But I just smiled up at him because I knew, good cop that Sarcovich was, he would never hit me. He knew it too, and that just made him even madder.

Why did I always go out of my way to annoy Sarcovich? That's easy to answer: he didn't like me. So why annoy him just because of that? After all, there are quite a few people in this world that don't like me and I don't try to annoy them. It's the reason he doesn't like me that bothers me. It's not because I ever did him an injustice, or ever botched a case badly (well, really badly!) when I was one of his detectives. No, the reason, or should I say reasons, are ones I have already mentioned. I am not from Pittsfield and some of the people of this city are close-minded. For people like Sarcovich, from a family that for generations has called Pittsfield home, it's one thing for outsiders to become simple officers on the police force. Who knows, after thirty or forty years of foot patrol you might actually come to be accepted. But to have the gall to receive promotion after promotion and actually become a detective was just too much for homegrown, good ol' boy Dave Sarcovich to stomach.

So the chief went out of his way to make my every waking moment on the force unbearable. He gave me every dirty assignment there was, assigned me every unsolvable case (some of which I solved). But did I gripe about that? Did I cave in and quit? Well, yes actually, but not until two years ago. That was when I handed in my badge, left the force and struck out on my own as a private investigator. And now here I was, about to work the same case as my old boss.

"Mr. Dunleavy is here at my request, Chief." The voice behind me was familiar, so I didn't jerk my head around to see who it was that spoke; instead I watched Sarcovich. He brought his eyes up over my head and looked directly at Mikah Johnston. I noticed the chief's upper lip curl in disgust. He had to play the game of politics with Johnston and he knew it. Sarcovich was not a political man. He was a straight shooter who disliked a lot of people and usually was free to show it. But with the movers and shakers of Pittsfield he had to be careful, and Mikah Johnston, as CEO of the largest single employer in Berkshire County, moved and shook things as much as anyone.

"You don't need a private investigator, Mr. Johnston," grumbled the chief, nodding towards me. "The police can handle this investigation."

"I'm sure you can, Chief. But Mr. Goodwin," said Johnston nodding to the figure on the floor, "was one of my employees and he was killed in my plant. There are obviously going to be internal inquiries that need to be, shall I say, kept from 'prying eyes.'"

"Prying eyes" was Johnston's name for the press. The three of us, Johnston, Sarcovich and I, knew that anything the police discovered in their investigation, whether it had anything to do with the murder or not, would eventually end up in the papers. And since no one knew where this investigation would lead, or to whom, it might prove useful to have certain avenues investigated by someone other than the police. That, at least, is what Johnston had told me on the phone early that morning after the discovery of the body.

Sarcovich saw that; you could tell from his expression he had seen it long before Johnston uttered it. You could also tell from his expression that he didn't appreciate the implications. It meant that I was going to be brought in on the case. He certainly didn't like that, but he was going to have to grit his teeth and accept it.

"Keep him out of the way," grunted the chief nodding towards me but still looking at Johnston. "You want him for 'internal inquiries,' just make sure they stay internal." Looking me straight in the eye, he added, "And don't expect anything from the police; no information, no manpower, no anything. You're on your own, Dunleavy." He turned back to where Fred was searching around the vending machines and walked away.

"Come on," said Johnston. "I've called the staff into my office and they're waiting for us." He turned, took a step or two, then stopped and turned back to me. "And wipe that grin off your face."

14

"Grin? What grin, Mikah?"

Johnston and I had been on a first name basis for several years. Six years earlier, when I was still on the force, we had been called in to find out who was sending bomb threats to Cyber Inc. The threats, which turned out to have been sent by a former disgruntled employee, were really a ruse to hide the fact that Johnston himself was the real target. I had caught the man just as he was setting a car bomb in Johnston's Mercedes. When I left the force later and was trying to set myself up as a private investigator, the grateful CEO brought me on board Cyber with a retainer, putting food on the table and leaving me free for other potential jobs.

"Listen, Barry, Sarcovich is a good cop and he'll keep the investigation moving along. If it was someone from outside the company who murdered Goodwin, Sarcovich will find them. But," he continued, stopping and grabbing my arm lightly to halt me as well, "if this has anything to do with Cyber or any of its employees, I want to know first. This is a very delicate time for us. We have several government contracts being negotiated, with the city and the state. The last thing I need is bad publicity making gun-shy politicians run for cover and leave us out in the cold. Do you understand?"

"I know the ground rules, Mikah, and I know why I'm here," I answered. "But you and I both know the odds are someone inside the company did this. Considering all the security around here, someone from the outside can't just waltz through the gates, kill an employee and waltz right back out."

Johnston let out a low sigh. "I know that, and you know that. And the chief probably knows that, too. Which means you have to find out what's going on before Sarcovich does."

Chapter 2

Mikah led me down the hall, threw a few left and right turns in for good measure, and we soon found ourselves in the board room. I had been there on a few other occasions to make presentations to the board of directors following my investigations. It had always been a crowded room then, probably because none of the bigwigs usually had anything to do with people in my profession and they needed something to brag about during that weekend's round of golf; I had been the hot item of discussion during those meetings. Now, however, I was just a working Joe going to meet with some of the other Joe's.

The room held only three people other than Johnston and myself. In the corner, standing by the large picture window that looked out on Silver Lake, was a tall woman, probably in her late thirties from the look of it. She was someone I had never met despite my frequent trips to Cyber Inc. Her black hair was cut to just above her shoulders, her sharp cheekbones softened just enough by strategically applied make-up. She wore a charcoal-gray business suit, and as she turned to face us I caught the sun glint off her jet-black eyes.

But there was something else about her that made me do a double take. There was coldness to her, a lack of softness in those eyes, a rigidness to her stance. Even from where I stood a room's length away, I could tell this was the kind of woman who could chew me up and spit me out given half a chance. I told myself not to give her that chance.

My eyes continued to take in the room, and they wandered to the large oak table in the middle of the floor. Seated one chair to the left of the table's head was someone I had met before. Donald ("call me Donny") Sackett was the vice president of sales, a smooth, glad-handing pitchman who could sell a corpse a lifetime ownership to a Florida condo. In his late forties I would guess, Sackett obviously kept in shape by working out. His chestnut-brown hair coiffed to perfection and his skin tanned, he exuded all the charm of a used car salesman. I could smell his abundant aftershave clear across the room. He was slick, but he did his job well and brought in the big bucks from clients all over the country. I knew Johnston wasn't crazy about the man, but Sackett kept the bottom line a lovely shade of black, so Mikah tolerated him.

Situated behind the head of the board table and to the left was a small but elegant desk. Seated at the desk was a tall and elegant woman. Our eyes met momentarily, then the woman turned to look back at her notebook on the desk. We didn't acknowledge each other's presence, but then we had already done so earlier that morning. Jenny St. Pierre was Mikah Johnston's administrative assistant. A tall, willowy blonde of thirty-three, Jenny was the sharpest knife in the drawer, no matter which drawer you dropped her in. She was strong-willed and efficient, a weapon Johnston couldn't do without and he knew it. She was also my on-again, off-again girl friend. Last night had been on-again. Come to think of it, so had earlier this morning.

"Everyone here?" said Mikah Johnston as we entered the room. "Good. Let's begin." He walked to the head of the table and sat down on one of the cushioned chairs. Forget the table, just one of the chairs probably cost more than my car.

Johnston motioned me to have a seat, but as he wasn't particularly specific with his wave I was left to choose my spot. I evidently chose wrong because just as I was about to grab for a chair the dark-haired woman, who had left her perch in front of the window, reached for the same one. Having remembered the promise made to myself three seconds earlier to stay out of the way of this woman, I tried to make the best of the situation. I pulled the chair out and said: "After you." The icy stare would have been more than enough to make me hightail it to safety, but her deep-throated "Thank you" really did it. As I moved to the other side of the table after she was seated, I cautiously checked my body for the knife wounds I knew had to be there.

"Barry, I know you've met Donny Sackett," he said as he indicated the used car salesman with his hand, "and I think you remember my administrative assistant, Jenny St. Pierre." Mikah knew of my relationship with Jenny; on several occasions Jenny and I had crossed paths with him while out after hours. I couldn't tell if he was being cute or just a gentleman. In any case it was irrelevant to the business at hand. Both Sackett and Jenny smiled and nodded. "But I don't believe you have had the opportunity to meet our vice president of finance, Samantha Macabee." He indicated the Ice Princess.

"I am well acquainted with Mr. Dunleavy," said the woman, a softness in her voice I had not expected.

"You are?" I asked. Despite the touch of frost adhering to her, she was beautiful, and I have a long memory for a good-looking woman. "I'm afraid I don't remember ever meeting..."

"We haven't met, but I know all about you. I'm the person who signs all your checks. You know, you can tell a lot about a person from the expense accounts they turn in to the company, and yours are, shall we say, unique," she said it with a smile, but the tone of voice she used made me want to check my body for more knife wounds. I made a mental note to stop including the bar tabs from Jake's in my expenses under the heading "Research."

"Well, now that we seem to have all met, let's get down to why we're here." Mikah shifted in his chair and looked at me. "Barry, the others have been apprised of the murder, but that's about all they, and I should add that I, know about the matter. Donny and Samantha have been told what your role in the investigation will be, and I have a teleconference scheduled with the directors later this morning to apprise them of the situation; I'm sure they will have no objections to your investigating the matter."

"I'm glad you're aboard, Barry," interrupted Sackett. "I don't have a lot of faith in Pittsfield's finest finding out what happened."

"You should," I replied. "They're not 'big city,' but they are efficient. Give them enough time and they'll find out the truth."

"As I told you before, Barry, time's the problem." It was Mikah again. "We're in the midst of several delicate negotiations with various government agencies. We don't want the investigation to linger too long; that will only spur gossip and innuendo about the company, and that's bound to hurt. On the other hand, we need a gentle approach with inquiries into the matter, and Chief Sarcovich is about as gentle as a bull elephant."

I smiled. Sarcovich was an excellent investigator, and the main reason was that he wasn't afraid of anyone or afraid to ask any question that needed to be asked. The problem was he didn't care who got upset. When you're dealing with big money and big politics, that's not good. Sarcovich was not going to be subtle, and Mikah Johnston wanted—and needed—subtle.

"As I told you earlier, Barry," continued Johnston, "I want you to handle the investigation as it applies internally to Cyber Inc. You'll have full access to all employees and all departments."

"Excuse me, Mr. Johnston." It was Samantha Macabee. "When you say 'all departments' I'm sure you don't mean financial. What with all the sensitive reports and the contracts we have in negotiations, I think…"

"I said all departments and that's exactly what I mean, Samantha." Mikah was smiling when he said it, but the tone of voice he used left no doubt he did, indeed, mean it.

Johnston could be as much a glad-hander as Sackett when he needed to be, but he was also the quintessential CEO. He was smart and hard; he had to be to have risen from a mere accountant with the company when he started with Cyber Inc. twenty-two years ago. He was only fifty-three, but in the four years since he had been elevated to Chief Executive he had quadrupled Cyber Inc.'s bottom line. And not only had he done it without laying off workers, he had created several hundred new jobs at the company. For a small city like Pittsfield, several hundred new tax-paying workers was quite a shot in the arm. The politicians in town loved him and most of his employees liked him. At this moment, however, I wasn't too sure about Samantha Macabee.

"Of course, sir," mumbled the woman. The she looked over to me. "Whatever you need, Mr. Dunleavy. My office is at your disposal. When you need something, see me personally and I'll see that you get it."

"Thank you, Ms. Macabee." I nodded. "I'll try to be as unobtrusive as possible." I turned back to Mikah Johnston. "And now, can we discuss the reason we're here: the victim?"

"His name was Larry Goodwin," volunteered Donny Sackett, leaning back in the plush chair. "He was a software engineer."

"Had he been here long?" I asked.

"Not very long," Sackett answered. "About ten months I would say."

"Nine months, fifteen days," interrupted Jenny. I looked over at her. She arose and walked over to me with a folder. She handed it to me then returned to her seat. How in the world could she make so simple a task look so sexy? I glanced through the papers in the folder, which turned out to be Goodwin's employment jacket.

"Let's see," I muttered aloud as I examined the papers in the folder. "Goodwin was only twenty-three years old."

"My God, what a waste," sighed Samantha Macabee. Might there actually be a heart under that nicely formed breast?

I continued my commentary on the documents. "Graduate of Worcester Polytechnic Institute, degree in Computer Science...." I stopped and looked up. "Wait a minute, is this Larry Goodwin, the All-American football player?"

"The one and only," chirped Sackett. "The kid had brains, good looks and was a star athlete. He was also supposed to have a great future. Oh well..." he shrugged, leaving the sentence unfinished.

"What were his duties here at Cyber Inc?" I asked, looking at Johnston. He merely looked over at his vice president of finance.

"Goodwin was getting his feet wet with the company, so we didn't assign him any of the major work," offered Macabee. "He was basically doing mop-up duty on some of the smaller projects. Since his work was at the end of the process, he was working pretty closely with Donny, so that everyone would be in step with marketing."

I turned back to Sackett. "So what was Goodwin like?"

"In what way? To work with, you mean?"

"We can start there. What about his personality? Was he super serious or did he joke around?"

"It would be hard for me to say," shrugged the salesman. "I was his superior and he was fresh out of college. He wasn't going to open up with me like he might with some of his coworkers. It was pretty apparent he knew his place in the food chain. He was deferential to me and just about every executive I saw him cross paths with."

"You didn't have any contact with him?" I asked, turning in my seat and facing Samantha Macabee. She seemed startled, by the suddenness of the question or the subject I wasn't sure.

"No," she answered, a little too loudly and a little too quickly. She caught herself. "I would see him around the plant, was in a few meetings where he was present, but nothing of any serious contact. His work and mine didn't mesh in any way. That is, except on payday"

"Did he do his job well?" I had turned back to Sackett and posed the question to him.

He gave a quick, furtive glance in Mikah Johnston's direction, then back at me. "More than competent. He was very bright, quick to pick up ideas. All you had to do was tell him something once and you got what you asked for."

"Any friction with coworkers?"

"None that I'm aware of."

Jenny broke in once more. "His jacket," she nodded towards the folder on the table in front of me, "doesn't show any complaints about him or from him regarding anyone else."

"Well that's just dandy," I said, closing the folder and throwing it about six inches away from me on the table. "We have a college hero, smart as a whip, good looking based on the ID photo in his folder, and liked by everyone. The only problem is he's lying on the floor dead."

"Actually," added Donny Sackett, "the most pressing problem is that he's lying on 'our' floor dead." He looked over toward Mikah Johnston, who gave Sackett a reproving look. Sackett didn't back down. "I'm sorry for how that sounds, Mikah. But we both know that a lot of hard work will go down the drain unless this mess gets cleared up in a hurry. That's why," he finished, looking at me, "I'm glad you're here to help."

Mikah Johnston sighed and stood up. Donny Sackett had said what the other two company executives had been thinking since earlier in the morning when the body had been discovered. It was Johnston's job to watch out for the welfare of the company and that meant being hard. Still, if I knew Mikah at all, he was thinking of finding a murderer, not crisis management.

"I think we've given Mr. Dunleavy enough to get started with," he said. He looked at me and nodded. I knew a dismissal when I saw one, so I stood up as well. "I have a conference call to make," he continued. "Samantha, I would like to see you and Donny in my office later. Make it about eleven o'clock."

If Samantha Macabee or Donny Sackett had any previous appointments set for eleven they weren't going to make them; even vice-presidents know how to take orders.

"Yes, Mikah," toned Macabee. She looked at me and smiled. "Well, Mr. Dunleavy, I'm sure we'll be seeing you around over the next several days." Fittingly, it had been a cold smile. She walked out of the room.

Sackett came over and stuck out his hand. "Good to have you aboard, Barry," he said, his smile much warmer but just as insincere as the woman's had been. I reached out and he grabbed my hand, giving it his best "deal closing" shake. "Let me know if you need anything in your investigation. By the way," he continued, reaching into his side coat pocket and bringing out something small and rectangular, "here's my card. Home phone number is on it, plus my cell phone. Just in case you need me after hours." He turned and also walked out of the room. I resisted the urge to smell my hand to see if the scent of his sickening after-shave had stuck to it.

As I watched Sackett leave the room, my eyes wandered over to the small desk Jenny had occupied during the meeting. She had spent the entire time taking down what had been said, and if I knew anything about her attention to detail that meant anyone reading the minutes would feel as if they had been in the room. Jenny was closing her notebook and straightening up, all just a little too slowly. It was obvious she was waiting for the room to clear of everyone but the two of us. I walked over smiling.

"Wipe the grin off your face, Dunleavy," she said, not returning my smile. "You have work to do and so do I. I suggest we both get to it." With that she turned on her heels and left me standing in the huge boardroom by myself. She had been waiting for us to be alone; it gave her a chance to put me in my place.

I walked out of the door to the meeting room, went down the hall and stopped at the elevator doors. I pushed the button and was waiting for the car when a voice behind me said, "I hope you catch the murderer quickly, Mr. Dunleavy."

I turned and came face to face with Samantha Macabee. Maybe the subdued lighting of the hallway softened her features, or maybe the soft tone of her voice startled me a little. Whatever the reason, she had a warmer, gentler look to her than had been the case in the conference room.

"I hope so too, Ms. Macabee," I answered.

"As I mentioned in the meeting, please feel free to ask for anything if you need help. Mr. Goodwin's killer cannot be allowed to get away with this horrible crime."

"I appreciate your offer, and I'm sure I'll take you up on it before long. After all, money is one of the two big reason people get murdered and you're the person to ask when it comes to money around here."

"I suppose I am," she answered thoughtfully, then added quickly, "although there's not much I can tell you about Mr. Goodwin's, or for that matter, any employee's, personal finances. I can only tell you what we pay, or should I say, paid him."

"Was it a substantial amount?"

"For a young man right out of college, yes, you could say it was substantial. But it was nowhere near what he would eventually make here. He was smart, competent and a go-getter. He had a great future with the company. Any amount of money that might have been involved in his death had to be peanuts."

"Perhaps," I semi-agreed. "We'll just have to see."

"By the way, you said money was only one of two reasons for murder. The other one would be?"

"Emotions," I answered. "Love, jealousy, hate, greed. If it wasn't money, one of those emotions, or another, has to fit into the murder somewhere. Even if money did play a role, so might emotion. When I find out, I'll be more than halfway to solving the crime."

"I guess you're right, Mr. Dunleavy," said Samantha Macabee in a somewhat subdued voice. "Anyway, please let me know when I can be of help."

"I'll do that, Ms. Macabee."

She turned and walked back down the hall. *She has a nice walk,* I told myself. But that wasn't the only thing I was thinking. If Samantha Macabee and Larry Goodwin had, in her own words in the meeting, "nothing of any serious contact," how did she know he was a "go-getter" and had a great future with the company? Was she just practicing the party line Johnston was ordering company executives to spew to the newspapers when asked? Or did she know Goodwin a little better than she let on?

Chapter 3

I decided to take Jenny's advice and get on with my investigation and soon I was headed across town to Larry Goodwin's apartment. I was working my way back up East Street, but having eluded death once that morning, and not feeling any more lucky than usual, I decided to avoid Park Square. I crossed over to Fenn Street, up First Street and then onto North Street. I was headed for the Springside section of town. It had surprised me when I looked in Goodwin's employee folder and saw his address.

Goodwin was young, single and pulling down good money as a computer software engineer with a large company. Also, his employee jacket stated that he had attended college on an athletic scholarship, so that meant no college loans to repay. Springside, for the most part, is a nice, comfortable residential area. There are, however, a few side streets in the neighborhood that could stand some renovation, or fumigation, or both. Goodwin was living on one of those streets, and that made me wonder why.

Several minutes later I pulled up outside the house I was looking for. Larry Goodwin rented a second floor flat in a two-family house. As I got out of my car, I looked around. Some of the other houses had cluttered front yards: old, stuffed living room chairs with slashed fabric; rusting metal tables; equally rusty bikes. In some neighborhoods you might have thought people were having a garage sale; in some of the ritzier neighborhoods they could have been putting things out for the junkman; here it was passing for lawn furniture. I locked my car and headed for the house.

As I approached the house I saw a car parked in the driveway. I walked over to it and saw a Cyber Inc. parking sticker on the rear passenger window. It was Goodwin's car all right, but the look of it shocked me. The car was old and run down, a perfect fit for the neighborhood but not for a young, college-educated computer whiz working for a big corporation. I gave the interior a quick look, but saw that the doors were locked. My glimpse showed me a neat and tidy car; no paper coffee cups lying around, no newspapers in the back seat, and no fast food bags on the floor. A more thorough search of the car would have to wait.

Goodwin's apartment, as I said, was on the second floor of the building. Since there was only one front door to the house I headed around the side looking for a staircase. I didn't find it until I got to the backyard. A wooden set of stairs without any handrail led to a bare metal door. I didn't have a key, so I walked over to what must have been the kitchen door of the first-floor apartment and knocked several times. There was no answer, and that was a problem. I knew Sarcovich would be sending his men to the apartment soon, or even worse, come himself; I had to hurry and get a good look at Goodwin's place before then. Nothing to do but go for it, I mentally shrugged to myself.

I took the old staircase two steps at a time. I intended to pick the lock. Having seen the rest of the house I assumed all I would need to get in was a pipe cleaner; but I was wrong. When I hit the second-floor landing I noticed that the door, which had looked old and rusted from down on the ground, was actually brand new, as were the locks. Plural! Three dead bolt locks made their way up the side of the door. Even had I been an expert at the kind of activity I had been planning, which I definitely am not, I knew I wouldn't have the time I needed.

"What d'ya know, Barry," came a voice from below the landing.

I looked down over the railing and saw Fred Martin. He was smiling back up at me. "I don't see you for weeks, and then we cross paths twice in one morning."

Fred was alone, but I looked from him towards the front of the house. "Sarcovich with you?"

"Nope. He stayed back at the station trying to get the autopsy of Goodwin moved to the front of the waiting list. And waiting to hear from me after I check the apartment."

"Right," I smiled. "Come on up."

"Now, Barry, you know the chief would have a fit if he found out I let you in on the search."

"Right," I smiled. "Come on up." He came up, a grin plastered on his face, and moments later, using the keys the police had taken from the victim's key ring earlier, we entered the flat.

To say that old phrase "you can't judge a book by its cover" applied here was an understatement. From the outside, the house looked dilapidated and run-down. Before we had entered the apartment I would have bet everything I owned that the inside would look about the same. But as we entered the building, Fred let out a low whistle.

"Would you look at this now," he muttered.

The room we were in looked about as high-tech as you could get. There were no stuffed chairs or sofas in sight; everything was metallic. But it was all sophisticated, trendy metallic furniture. New and expensive furniture! There were two seven-foot tables in front of us: one on the opposite wall and another, butted up against the first, on the adjacent wall. On both tables were an assortment of computers, printers, scanners and other types of computer hardware I was not familiar with. Whatever Goodwin was saving on the rent for this dump he was putting into computer hardware. In front of one of the tables was an expensive-looking office chair on rollers.

A quick look around the rest of the room showed a kitchenette to the right, but no kitchen table. Our boy obviously ate in front of the computer screen and not the television, since there wasn't one in sight. There was a door in the far right corner of the room and Fred moved over to it quickly. He slid his hand around the doorframe and a light came on in the next room.

"Bedroom," he called over his shoulder to me. "More or less."

I walked over to the doorway and looked in. Fred would have been correct in his description of the room, had there been a bed in sight. Rather there was only a mattress with a couple of blankets and a pillow lying on top.

"He still had a college-boy mentality," I said. "Sleeping on the floor still had some appeal to him."

The two of us crossed over to yet another door, this time situated on the right-hand wall of the bedroom. Once again, Fred turned on the light. It was the bathroom, and my former partner lost no time in rummaging through the medicine cabinet.

"Typical," he said as he went through the inventory. "Deodorant, shaving cream, other hygiene articles." He walked over to the bathtub. It was a combination shower-tub and he pulled back the shower curtain. After a second, he said, "Nothing much here. Let's get back to those computers."

Fred turned and walked past me as I pretended to look at the contents of the medicine cabinet. Once I was alone in the room, I quickly crossed to the bathtub and ran my hand over the porcelain surface. It was dry. As I was passing the sink on my way out, I rubbed my hand across the surface of that as well; it was also dry. Goodwin hadn't used either for a while, which meant he hadn't been home for some time. *Fred must be getting old*, I thought, and I made a mental note to bring up the point after this case was finished. But for now, all I did was follow my ex-partner back to the living room and the computers.

"How much do you figure this stuff is worth?" he asked as I crossed to meet him at the two large tables.

"Got me," I answered with a shrug. "I'm not an expert on this stuff."

"I thought you were the 'modern cop' on the force." He laughed. "At least you seemed to know what was going on in the world; seem to keep up on all the newest things."

"Well, I know how to turn them on and I can run a few programs. As a matter of fact, I just bought a computer for the office a few months ago. It ran about seven hundred, but that was on sale at one of those computer stores. These things," I indicated the machines on the tables, "are state of the art. These two desktop models have 19-inch flat screens, the scanners are big-time, and those two printers have to run about two thousand dollars each. This laptop goes for three grand easy. You're looking at twelve or fifteen grand sitting on these tables."

Fred let out that low whistle once more. "Well, you have to figure he needed this stuff, being a computer engineer for Cyber and all. And he made enough money to buy it if he wanted. The question is why was he living in a dump like this? And he knew he wasn't living in the best neighborhood in Pittsfield. He's got three deadbolt locks on a steel door; nobody was breaking in here."

I walked over to the computer situated in front of the leather office chair. I touched it, feeling a metal cover completely cold to the touch. Reaching down the length of the table I put my other hand on the second computer. Nodding toward the first machine, I said to Fred, "These machines are cold. They haven't been running for a while. But the laptop is open. Goodwin wouldn't have left the top up if he thought he'd be gone long. As a matter of fact, he probably would have taken it with him."

"Can you turn it on?" asked Fred.

"Here we go," I answered. I reached out and pushed in the "On" button. I turned back toward my former partner. "This will take a few seconds to boot up the operating system. In the meantime…"

"Hey, what's that?" interrupted Fred, pointing to the monitor.

I spun around quickly, but all I saw was the black screen booting up. "What's what?"

"The monitor was acting funny. It was going through its usual computer garbage, then suddenly a big letter 'I' shot up on the screen."

"I didn't see anything. Besides," I continued, "it's not there now."

"I can see that, Mr. Private Eye," Fred answered sarcastically. "But it was there a second ago. Restart it and see for yourself."

I shrugged, and turning back to the computer hit the restart button. The monitor screen went black, and then a few seconds later started booting up. This time I kept my eyes glued to the screen. Sure enough the boot sequence was interrupted by the appearance of a capital 'I' plastered in the middle of the screen. It was there for only one or two seconds, then disappeared in the rush of computer gibberish.

"Hey! What are you guys doing here? Who are you?"

Fred and I both wheeled toward the door at the sound of the voice. Fred's hand instinctively went to his hip where he carried his service revolver in its holster. My hand would have done the same except I don't have a holster. Or a gun, for that matter. I didn't see a need for one in my line of work. Even on the force I was usually able to talk my way out of trouble. Come to think of it, it was my gift of gab that annoyed Sarcovich about as much as anything.

A man in a ratty T-shirt and dirty jeans was standing in the doorway leading from the landing. He obviously needed a shave, and if I took another step or two in his direction I would probably discover he needed a bath as well. Fred relaxed a little, stuck his hand in his coat pocket and produced a badge.

"Police," he mumbled. "Who are you?"

"Tre Barker," answered the man, suddenly looking disconcerted. I had seen his kind plenty of times when I was on the force: a tough guy who suddenly went soft when he was facing the cops. "I own this building. I live in the downstairs apartment." He hesitated, then asked, "Goodwin in trouble? Figured it was only a matter of time."

"Why's that?" I asked.

"Look at the door. Guys with nothing to hide don't live behind steel doors with locks out the wazoo. And they don't get late-night visitors on a regular basis."

"What visitors?"

"How do I know? Do I look like his social secretary? Besides, most of his visitors didn't look like they wanted to socialize, if you know what I mean."

"No, we don't," said Fred. "Why don't you tell us?"

The man suddenly had a nervous look on his face. "Look," he

said after a second, "in this neighborhood you pretty much keep your nose out of other people's business, ya know? I don't want any trouble."

"From who?" Fred egged the man on.

Barkers looked from Fred to me then back to Fred. He sighed. "Look, you didn't hear this from me, okay?" He looked over his should at the landing, as if someone were hiding there just to listen in on the conversation, then he turned back to face us. "Two guys. Two big guys. They would come around about once a week for the last several months. I recognized them."

"Who were they?" I asked. There was no immediate answer, just a look on the man's face as though he was in the midst of making up his mind whether to say anymore, so I asked again. "Who were they?"

"Vinnie Lombardi's boys," he said finally, but very quickly and quietly.

"How do you know they work for Lombardi?" asked Fred.

"I work in North Adams," answered Barker. "Every once in awhile I'll place a little bet with Vinnie. I recognized his boys."

"So you like to play with bookies, huh?" said Fred, the policeman in him coming out.

"Hey, look," said Barker smiling, but obviously not very happy, "what's the matter with a little bet on a basketball game every now and then? Who's it going to hurt?"

"According to you," I interrupted, "Goodwin may have been hurt."

"He got hurt?"

"He got dead," said Fred, taking a step closer toward the man. "And now we find out Vinnie Lombardi is involved in the dead man's life."

Barker's face dropped and he backed up quickly, but only got as far as the wall. "Dead?" he almost shouted. "And you think Vinnie…and you had me rat on him?"

The man was losing any grip he may have had on his nerves when he entered the room, and Fred wasn't about to let up on him. As a former cop, I knew this was when the best information was liable to come out.

"When was the last time Vinnie's goons were here? Come on! When?" Fred was in Barker's face and the latter man was starting to shake.

"I don't know, honest."

"Look," I said, stepping between Fred and Barker. "I know you're afraid of Lombardi. I don't blame you. But you're already in this as a witness. You might as well tell everything. That way we can get Lombardi and the police can protect you. If you won't say anything, then we'll walk out of here and start our own investigation. And when Lombardi hears you're the one who started us on his trail, you'll be on your own without any police help."

Barker just stood there for a few moments quivering. You could see from the look in his eyes he was thinking things through, the way a cornered animal looks for a means of escape. He knew he had said too much, but he also knew he couldn't take any of it back. Going ahead all the way would be his only way out. He made his decision.

"Two nights ago. Vinnie's boys were here two nights ago."

"Was Goodwin here?"

"I don't think so. I haven't seen him around here for the past three or four days. But that doesn't mean anything. Like I said, I work in North Adams. He could have been here while I was at work. It would have been safer for him in the daytime anyway. More people around, more witnesses."

Fred looked at me and I nodded slightly. The man had told the truth and put us on a hot lead.

"Come on," said Fred to Tre Barker, grabbing his arm and swinging him around to face the door. "I think you should come to the station with me."

"What for?" the man complained. "I've been helpful. I answered your questions!"

"But not all of them. I have more I want to ask at headquarters. Besides, you'll be safer there."

The word "safer" seemed to ease the tension in Barker's face a little and he went out the door and down the stairs somewhat more calmly than he had been in the room.

I walked back to the computer and shut it down. There would be time later to check out the files on the hard drive. I had no illusions about me doing the checking; the boys down at police headquarters would do that. But, once again, somebody would fill me in.

Fred, keeping hold of Barker's arm, escorted him to the police car and placed Barker in the backseat. Slamming the door, the policeman faced me. "That Goodwin's car over there?" he asked, nodding toward the old vehicle in the drive.

"Yeah," I answered. "It's locked, so I haven't had a chance to check it out."

"I'll get a police tow up here and have it brought to the impound lot. I'll also get another crew to get the computer equipment brought in." He walked around to the driver's door of the squad car, stopped and looked at me. "You're not going to do anything stupid, are you?" he asked, not smiling.

"Like what?" I replied innocently.

"Like taking a scenic drive up Route 8 to North Adams."

"I wasn't planning on it, but since you mentioned it, I hear MassMoca has a new exhibit opening. Might be worth the drive to take a look."

"And it might be worth your health not to. Look, Barry, you're not a cop anymore. You go walking into Vinnie Lombardi's place without a badge to back you up and you might not walk back out. Lombardi is bad news."

"Fred, I agree with you. There are very few things in this world that would make me visit Vinnie Lombardi."

"Promise you won't go?"

"I promise."

He smiled. "Good. If everything goes okay, I should be off duty at four o'clock. Meet me at Jake's for a beer." He walked around the car to the driver's side, got in, started the engine and drove off with Tre Barker in the backseat looking very worried.

Ten minutes later I was on Route 8 heading for North Adams. Okay, I lied to Fred. I knew I was lying when I made the promise, but

Fred probably knew I was lying as well. That's why he made it a point to have me meet him at Jake's. I would make it up to him by buying a beer. Or two.

Chapter 4

Living in the Berkshires of western Massachusetts can be idyllic enough to make Adam and Eve green with jealousy. You get to mix city comforts with rustic beauty. Drive approximately twelve minutes north from downtown Pittsfield and you'll find yourself in the greenest, most luscious countryside you've ever seen. My trip to North Adams meant a nice, contemplative drive up Route 8, not necessarily the most scenic of trips in the Berkshires but a lot better than most roads I can think of. If the quiet and the beauty don't help you clear your head then you are definitely in the need of strong medication.

But the only time it would even remotely occur to me to drive north along this route was during April; the rest of the year it is crawling with tourists, all of them trying to avoid Route 7, which also travels north. In winter, the skiers can't decide whether to stop at one of the local ski mountains or continue on to Vermont; in autumn, the "leaf peepers" come from all over the world to look at our maple trees turn color (which are basically the same color the maple trees outside their homes are turning at exactly the same time); and in the summer, Route 8 is awash in people traveling south who want to take in the Boston Symphony Orchestra at its summer home at Tanglewood in Lenox, or north to check out the big stars appearing at the Theater

Festival in Williamstown. Fortunately for me, this just happened to be one of those few weeks out of the year it was safe to travel the road.

It was a weekday morning in the spring, so I had the road to myself. That sweet fragrance I had managed to barely catch on my drive across West Street in Pittsfield was now a full bloom that filled my car and my head. The sun beat down and the wind rushing into my open car window blew my hair. I cruised through Lanesboro and into (and almost immediately out of) the town of Adams. Route 8 soon became Curran Highway and before I knew it I was in North Adams. So much for time to contemplate the scenic wonders of the Berkshires.

How does one describe the city of North Adams? When I first moved to the Berkshires, the city had the warranted reputation as the armpit of Massachusetts. A mill town that had lost its mills, and just about everything else of value, North Adams was slowly working its way from the bottom of the heap downward. Then a miracle occurred. A group of investors saw an old electric plant abandoned and envisioned it becoming a world-class art museum. You're probably wondering the same thing we did in Pittsfield: where are these people getting their drugs? But out of that warped psychedelic haze came MassMoca, the Massachusetts Museum of Contemporary Art. Tourist flocked from all over the world to little North Adams. The city cleaned up the streets and turned on the lights. So I guess the saying is true, after all: if you build it, they will come. And it doesn't make any difference what "it" is. Somebody always comes, and they are known as tourists.

The only problem with going from the bottom of the heap upward is that sometimes people you wish would get off at the next stop don't. They hang on, hoping to get something out of the ride. And the people who wish they would get off are the same people who never did anything about them when the city was down and out. Vinnie Lombardi was the kind of person you wish had never come along for the ride.

MassMoca is in the heart of the city and so is Vinnie. His business of record, the IRS record, is a diner two blocks removed the world-famous art museum, and is imaginatively called "Vinnie's Diner." I turned off Route 8 onto the main drag and quickly found a parking spot a few doors down from the diner. I stopped the car, got out, and figuring North Adams would never lose its original charm no matter how big or famous it became, locked the car doors.

The museum parking lot had looked packed as I drove by it, and the spillover from its clientele onto the city streets made it a little difficult to get to the diner quickly. A group of old ladies, obviously part of one of the numerous New England bus tours the Berkshires are so famous for, was crowded around the front window of an antique store (another thing the Berkshires are famous for) and didn't look like they planned on moving anytime soon. I didn't have any real concerns about going to confront a bookie and his goons, but I had learned very early in my years on the police force never to fool with old ladies; they're tough. So I did the chivalrous thing and stepped into the gutter of the street in order to walk around the group. My good deed was rewarded by one of the ladies who, glancing at me as I stepped off the sidewalk and into the street, smirked in such a way as to say "That's where you belong, buddy," and returned her attention to the antique store window. So much for chivalry!

As I entered the diner, I was surprised to see how clean and modern everything looked. I had been in the place once before, about five years earlier when I was still a detective on the force. A Pittsfield native had signed out a complaint alleging that Vinnie's men had come to his house one night to "request" that he pay a bill somewhat overdue. In cooperation with the state police, I had come to the diner to investigate the allegation. Back then it was a real dump, even for pre-Renaissance North Adams. But it looked like either the city had gotten Vinnie to clean up the building or he did it on his own to try and cash in on the tourist crowd. If that was the case, Vinnie might have made a costly mistake: there was no one in the place except for Vinnie and two of his goons, sitting in a booth by the window, and a nondescript waitress behind the counter. I crossed to the booth.

"Hello, Vinnie. Remember me?" My tone of voice was pleasant and light. I didn't care if the bookie was nice back; I was just interested in getting some kind of reaction I could play off.

Vinnie was a large man. Actually, Vinnie was fat! A lifetime of sitting around collecting bets and having others do your dirty work for you doesn't do much for one's physique. He looked hard at me, gave a quick half-frown and then shot his eyebrows up in surprise.

"Barry Dunleavy, formerly of the Pittsfield police force. Didn't I hear you quit a while back? You're some kind of private detective now." He turned to look across the booth at his two helpers and grinned. "What do you think, boys? This guy fancies himself a private eye." He gave a little laugh. There must have been a joke in there somewhere and I must have missed it because the two muscle men of Vinnie's started cackling.

I bent down and quickly looked under the table, then stood up straight.

"That's pretty good, Vinnie. I don't see any strings, yet you made two dummies move their mouths and laugh. How did you do that?"

If I had entered the diner looking for a reaction I could run with, I got it. And it was the one I had hoped for. The two goons got the insult pretty quickly and made a move to get up from the booth. I could have saved myself a lot of trouble had I simply smacked down the first man before he could stand; that would have prevented the second enforcer from getting out. But I wanted Vinnie to know who he was dealing with; it would make getting information out of him easier. I backed up to let the two men, both of whom were larger than myself and a good thirty pounds heavier, stand up freely. Vinnie took my retreat as a sign of fear.

"You shouldn't have started something you can't finish, Dunleavy. Now my boys are going to have to finish it for you." He shook his head as he said it, as if in mild rebuke of my words. But he said it with a large grin on his face.

I remember once when I was still on the police force and was visiting the local community college, giving a talk to a group of criminal justice students. During the question and answer period after my little speech I was asked what I thought was the most important quality in a police officer. I answered that I thought a good cop had a strong sense of what he could and could not do as an individual. Basically, you had to know your limitations. I bring that up because at this point you may be thinking that I was a little full of myself, trying to take on two professional leg-busters.

I was in the military for fours years, two-and-a-half of which were spent in the military police. Since I was stationed at a Marine base, my main function was to handle drunken Marines on weekends. The people in charge know that's going to be your main focus so they train you for it. Now a drunken Marine may be drunk, but he is still a Marine. They usually don't weigh as much as either of the two goons standing in front of me at the moment, but they are stronger, faster and have been trained to kill with their bare hands. I was trained to not only protect myself in situations with Marines, but also handle the situation and stop the Marine. I wasn't too worried about the up-coming events.

The first guy out of the booth almost made it to a full standing position before my right foot met his groin. The look of shock on his face didn't last long as the heel of my right palm met his left temple and he fell sideways to the floor. That gave his friend time to slide all the way out of the booth, stand and let fly a massive, but flabby fist in the direction of my face. I brought my left arm up and grabbed the wrist of the in-coming blow, at the same time twisting to my left so I stood sideways to my attacker. Since throwing the blow was taking the man off balance somewhat, I helped matters along by pulling on the wrist and dragging the man into me. At the same time, I brought up my right elbow and thrust it hard into the bridge of the man's nose. He would have fallen backwards, but I still had the wrist. I twisted the arm outward, taking the goon off-balance once more and bringing him to the floor. A well-aimed kick, and the man was on the floor holding his crotch and bleeding profusely from his nose. It had all unfolded in six seconds. I looked down at Vinnie, still seated at the booth. He wasn't smiling anymore, but I was as I sat down across from him.

"Okay, so you're tough," he growled. "What do you want?"

"Just a little information," I answered.

"Buy a newspaper."

My hand came up fast, so fast Vinnie never saw it coming. It crossed the bookie's face with a loud smack.

"Save the wise crap for somebody who appreciates it," I said, this time the tone in my voice anything but friendly. I knew that what I had just done amounted to assault on a private citizen, but I also knew Vinnie wasn't going to report it to the local police. "Just answer my questions and I'll leave. Otherwise, I'll stay around a while longer."

Vinnie rubbed the cheek that had been slapped, but he knew all the rubbing in the world wasn't going to get rid of the embarrassment he had just suffered before his men and the waitress. I made a mental note that he would probably want to do something about that in the future, and then I continued.

"What do you know about a Larry Goodwin?"

"Never heard of him," Vinnie grumbled, still rubbing his face.

I brought my right hand up once more, this time slower so the bookie could see it coming. He brought his hands up in front of his face and pushed back into the booth.

"Wait! Wait!" I brought my hand down. Vinnie relaxed and straightened up a little. "Okay, I know Goodwin. We do a little...business every once in awhile."

"How much business and how often?"

"Often enough to make Goodwin a regular. The kind of regular I like." He gave a little smile.

"That mean's the kind of regular who loses regularly, right?"

Vinnie nodded his head. "Regularly and big. He didn't believe in ten dollar bets."

"How much is he in to you for?" I asked.

"One hundred and fifteen thousand," Vinnie grinned back. "I'm planning on using it to take a cruise."

"You must want to leave pretty soon, since you've been sending your boys to roust him for the money."

"That why you're here? Goodwin hire you?" The bookie had a look in his eye like the man who's prized songbird got out of its cage and had flown away. Vinnie saw his cruise ship sailing without him.

"Look, Dunleavy. Goodwin played the game and he lost fair and square. He owes, that means he pays."

"Relax," I said. "Goodwin didn't hire me." Vinnie looked at me closely for a moment, then got his grin back. That's when I added, "Goodwin didn't hire anybody. He's dead."

The bookie's face went white fast, so fast that the thought of Lombardi losing his lunch all over me crossed my mind. Vinnie was a thug, and not above using a little force to get his way, or his money. But in the bookie business it wasn't too bright to lower your client base. Vinnie wasn't a murderer, and I had known it ever since Tre Barker tried to put Fred and I on Lombardi's tail. Vinnie wanted Goodwin's money, not his life. Goodwin was only worth something to Vinnie alive. Now, he was worth nothing.

"How long had Goodwin been doing business with you?"

"About six months," Lombardi mumbled, obviously still in mourning over his lost debt.

I had just wanted to clear up a few points and Vinnie had done that. It was time to leave. I slid out of the booth and stepped over the two goons. They were sitting up, but Vinnie had motioned them earlier not to get off the floor. I walked to the door, then stopped and turned around.

"No hard feelings, Vinnie," I said with a smile.

Lombardi rubbed his cheek as his men got to their feet. "Feelings are for suckers, Dunleavy," the bookie replied. Then that smile crossed his face again. "It's actions that count."

"A famous man once said," I smiled back, "'Revenge is a kind of wild justice.'"

"What the hell does that mean?"

"It means that you should just finish your lunch and forget about what happened in here today. Now that you're not taking that cruise, you need to look after your health. And Pittsfield is not really a healthy place to be these days." I turned and walked out.

I returned to my car and found that things really hadn't changed too much in North Adams. I had a parking ticket on my windshield. I looked closely at it and saw that I had been parked in a 30-minute zone for (and here I checked my watch) exactly thirty-four minutes. Oh well, I sighed as I got in my car. The information I got from Vinnie was certainly worth the entire ten bucks the ticket would run me. As I drove away from the curb, I wondered to myself how I could write it up on my expense account. Then I remembered Samantha Macabee and I figured I would just eat the fine.

Rather than head directly back to Pittsfield, I decided that since I had made the trip to North Adams I might as well drop in on an old friend. I turned the car around and headed down the street a few blocks to the North Adams Police Department. Upon reaching my destination, I stopped the car, got out and locked the doors (I was still in North Adams, after all). I went inside and asked to see Sergeant Brian Miller. Miller and I had served on a county task force several years earlier, struck up a friendship and had actually kept in touch with each other.

"Barry!" called Brian as he walked down the stairs from his office a few minutes later and spotted me. He came over and we shook hands."How have you been? I haven't heard from you since that Christmas card you sent the wife and I."

"I'm fine, Brian. It's good to see you. I came to town on a little business, and since I was in the neighborhood I thought I would stop by."

"To get a little information?" he asked smiling.

"Yes," I admitted, "but also to say hello."

"Is this information you're looking for going to require me to sort through our records?"

"Well, since you've been on the force over twenty years I'm willing to bet you can give the lowdown off the top of your head."

"Good! That means we can go outside and sit in the fresh air. It's too nice of a day to be cooped up inside."

We went outside, grabbed an open bench in front of the police station and made ourselves comfortable.

"So what kind of information are you looking for, Barry?"

"I need a little background on Vinnie Lombardi."

"Lombardi?" Brian said, a frown making its way across his brow.

"He's bad news, Barry. You sure you want to tangle with him?"

"I have no choice, Brian. There's been a murder in Pittsfield and Lombardi's name has come up in connection with the victim."

"Murder? I didn't hear anything about a murder."

"It just happened early this morning. It will be all over the newspapers and TV later today. So how about a little lowdown?"

"Well, it's funny you should be asking about Vinnie right now," said Brian, leaning back on the bench and stretching his lanky six-foot-three-inch frame out.

"Why's that?"

Well, you know North Adams has been going through what the local media likes to call a 'renaissance.' What you may not know is that the word has come down that in order to keep the renaissance going, it would be a good idea to get rid of as many 'undesirables' as possible."

"Undesirables like Vinnie Lombardi, you mean."

"Exactly. To that end, the force has been digging a lot deeper into Lombardi's doings than we have in the past. Oh, we knew he was making book and we would investigate anytime a citizen would complain Vinnie was too rough collecting an outstanding debt. But once we started looking harder, we found out that Vinnie's net was cast a lot further than we thought."

"You mean he's into more than just loan sharking and gambling?"

"No, I mean his loan sharking and gambling empire extended further than we thought. For example, we found out that his gambling business has a large base at the college."

"The college? You mean the Massachusetts College of Liberal Arts?"

"That's the only college in town, Barry. It seems that as far back as fifteen years ago, back when MCLA was still called 'North Adams State,' Lombardi was getting students hooked on the gambling bug. He has a built-in clientele. The college never runs out of students, and the older ones are indoctrinating the freshman into the ways of gambling. Since Vinnie is the only book in town, he's got something of a monopoly going."

"Yeah, but how much can he be making off college kids. They are notoriously low on funds."

"You haven't been to college in a while, have you? College kids today have a lot more disposable income than we had. We're talking a lot of money to be had, and Lombardi is not shy about going after his share. And now that the city is starting to pick up, there's a bigger piece of the pie waiting for someone to take it. "

I didn't say anything for a moment or two. "Well, Brian, you've given me something new to chew on." We stood up and shook hands.

"So when are we going to have you over for dinner, Barry?"

"Soon, Brian. I promise."

I turned and started walking to my car. My head was turning around the facts as I knew them, in no particular order. I tried to make some semblance of sense out of them. Larry Goodwin liked to gamble and he was just out of college. But he hadn't gone to MCLA where Lombardi was a gambling presence. But Goodwin was in debt to Lombardi. But Lombardi says he didn't know Goodwin was dead. But! But! But!

Chapter 5

The weather had not changed one bit since my trip up Route 8, so the return was just as pleasant, only this time I actually had some real information to chew on. Trc Barker had put me onto Vinnie, and in the landlord's petty little mind he probably thought the bookie was a good bet for the murder. But I had known better, and my trip to North Adams was more to verify what I had been thinking ever since Vinnie Lombardi's name had come up.

Why does a young hotshot computer programmer, working in a billion dollar business and making good money, choose to live in a dump in one of the worst sections of town? Why does the apartment have thousands of dollars worth of computer equipment in it, but almost no furniture? Why are there more locks on his crummy apartment door than in Fort Knox? The answer is simple, especially when a bookie is added to the equation: Goodwin had a gambling problem, and from the sound of it, a big gambling problem. And he was in hock to Vinnie for one hundred and fifteen grand. He couldn't afford a better apartment. He probably sold his furniture and anything else he had that was worth anything. If I bothered to look really hard I could probably find his college ring in some pawnshop. But Goodwin was a computer geek. He couldn't, or wouldn't, part with the computers, monitors, scanners and other hardware. So he went into hiding, trying to stay as far away from Vinnie Lombardi's goons as he could. He bought deadbolt locks by the gross to keep him safe when he couldn't hide and it hadn't helped.

Larry Goodwin had died inside the Cyber Inc. corporate offices. Vinnie and his goons couldn't have gotten into that building in a million years. That meant Vinnie didn't kill Goodwin, but it didn't necessarily eliminate the one hundred and fifteen thousand dollar debt as a motive for the killing. In fact, I was sure it was at the heart of the whole sordid mess.

It was only a little past one p.m. by the time I arrived back in Pittsfield, too early to meet Fred Martin and/or Sammy Brackens at Jake's Tavern. I thought this might be a good time to check out Larry Goodwin's office at Cyber Inc. As I rolled up to the gate of the plant, the guard from earlier that day, obviously still on duty, put his hand out to stop me. He probably only waved through the guests when he got the word from upstairs, like this morning. I stopped and rolled down the window.

"How ya doing?" I smiled. He didn't smile back. After an awkward second or two of his merely staring at me, I added, "Dunleavy, Barry."

The guard checked his list. I obviously wasn't there because he had to flip to the back sheet on his clipboard.

"Dunleavy," he mumbled to himself, and everyone else within twenty yards, as he scanned his list. "Dunleavy, Dunlea…here you are." He looked up. "Should have said you were on the 'revolving list.'"

"I would have had I known I was on the 'revolving list.' But then, I don't even know what a 'revolving list' is."

"It means you can come into the plant anytime you want, day or night. You won't be on any of the daily lists, so whenever you show up from now on just tell the guard on duty."

"Thanks, I'll do that." It was time to play detective, so I said, "Say, in all the time I've been coming here I never got your name."

"Jackson." The man smiled for the first time. He obviously was glad somebody had taken the time to get his name, maybe for the first time since he began working at Cyber. "Tim Jackson."

I stuck my hand out of the open car window; Jackson took it and gave it a firm shake. "Nice to meet you, Tim. Listen, how long have you been on duty today?"

"I came on duty at six a.m., start of the first shift. I'll be on until two p.m."

"I take it you heard about what happened inside?"

"Yep," he nodded. "Just about everyone at the company has. Word's come down not to talk to anyone about it, though." Then he leaned down and crossed his elbows on the doorframe and smiled. "That wouldn't include you, though, Mr. Dunleavy. Mr. Johnston gave orders for everybody to cooperate with you and answer all your questions. So, shoot!"

"Thanks," I smiled back. "And it's 'Barry,' not 'Mr. Dunleavy.' Did Larry Goodwin show up after you came on duty this morning?"

"Nope. I haven't seen Mr. Goodwin since he drove up to the gates yesterday morning around 6:45 a.m."

"He always showed up to work that early?"

"Sometimes earlier, but never later. When I worked third shift I'd sometimes check him out around midnight."

"How long has it been since you last worked the late shift?" I asked.

"Not since early December. I worked a couple of double shifts to get a little extra spending money for the holidays."

"And Goodwin always left work late?"

Jackson nodded. "And always came back early. I swear that boy had no social life at all."

"Just him and his computers, huh?"

"You got it," laughed the guard. "And him this good looking young guy, good job, great future. You figure it."

"Well, that's what I'm here to do. Thanks for the information, Tim. I may need to talk to you again later."

"Anytime, Barry. Take it easy."

I drove up to the corporate headquarters building that I had left just a few hours earlier, once again pulling into the visitor's parking section. I entered the building and walked up to the receptionist. She was a pretty nineteen- or twenty-year-old, obviously new to the job. I could tell because she looked up and gave me a pleasant smile rather than a fake, obligatory one. Hey, thats why I'm a detective; I have an eye for these things.

"Excuse me," I smiled back, "can you direct me to Larry Goodwin's office?"

The smile left her face fast, very fast. "I'm sorry," she managed to get out after a second's hesitation, "did you say 'Larry Goodwin'?"

"That's right," I answered, still smiling. "Larry Goodwin."

"I'll check that for you, sir," she said as she reached for the phone. "May I have your name, please?"

"It's Barry Dunleavy," came a voice from behind me. I turned and saw Donny Sackett approaching from the other end of the hallway. "Don't worry about checking with anyone, Rhonda," he said to the young receptionist. "Mr. Dunleavy has complete freedom around the entire plant, Mr. Johnston's orders."

Sackett reached out his hand and I shook it, once again wondering if scent can rub off on people.

"Why don't you follow me, Barry? I'm headed in that direction."

"Thanks," I answered. I fell in with Sackett, working hard to keep up with the salesman. It wasn't that his stride was long; he just kept moving his legs quicker than most people do. Like all salesmen, he was always on the go.

"So how's the investigation going?" Sackett asked before we went twenty feet.

"Interestingly," I answered in a noncommittal tone. At this early stage of the game, I wasn't about to give out more information to anyone than I had to. "I hear Goodwin was a hard worker."

"Depend on what you mean by 'hard.'" Sackett smiled.

"He came in early and left late."

"That might mean he worked 'long,' not 'hard.' Like I said this morning, Larry was new, he was learning the ropes. He had to work a little longer on a project than a more experienced guy would have. But he stuck with it and got the work done, so I'd have to agree that he was a 'hard worker.'"

"So you think that's the reason he worked all that extra time: he couldn't get the work done otherwise?"

The salesman shrugged. "Look, I didn't have all that much daily contact with Larry. All I know is that when I needed something from him when a deadline was up, the answer was 'I'll have that for you in an hour or two,' not 'I have that right here waiting for you.' It would slow me up a little, but it never cost us a contract."

"I thought you said this morning that he was a quick learner. You would ask him for something once and he would get it to you."

Sackett stopped his power walk and turned to face me. "Look, Barry, I didn't want to put the kid down this morning in front of Mikah. He was big on Goodwin; it was Mikah who pushed us into hiring him."

"So Goodwin wasn't the hot shot computer whiz everyone made him out to be?"

"He knew his stuff on a computer; at least I guess he knew his stuff. I don't know squat about computers; all I can do on the thing is write a letter. What I said this morning was true; he didn't need to be told anything twice. But he was having trouble getting the work done on schedule. I don't know why. The work wasn't that difficult or complicated. I was beginning to think that he had something going on outside of Cyber that kept him from getting his work done on time."

I didn't buy that. What could he have going on outside of his job if he was at the plant every day from six a.m. until midnight? Then again, maybe what he had going on outside of his job wasn't necessarily outside of the plant. Now more than ever I wanted to get a look at Goodwin's office. Sackett and I started walking again and in a few seconds we reached it.

It was a small office, befitting a new low-level computer geek in a multinational corporation. The furniture, while not new, was the top-of-the-line brand. The carpet had a cigarette burn here and there and was starting to fade in patches from the sun. How the sun ever got in, I don't know. The only window in the room had a northwesterly exposure. And the size of the room was another problem. If you could fit more than two people in the room at one time it was because at least one of them was a midget. No room to socialize and no aesthetics to attract a crowd. Most people would have suffocated in this office, but to a computer whiz like Goodwin it probably felt like he had died and gone to heaven.

"Thanks for guiding me here," I said to Sackett. "I think I can handle it now."

"No problem. Let me know if I can be of further help."

I nodded and turned back toward the office. The desk was on the far wall, just below the window. The computer monitor was sitting on the desk with the computer itself on the floor next to it. I crossed the room, sat in the green cushioned swivel chair and powered up the machine.

"What are you hoping to find?" asked Sackett from the doorway.

I thought the man would have taken the hint when I thanked him and he had gone about his business. Obviously he felt his business and mine were the same. I didn't bother to turn toward him, instead continuing to watch the monitor as I spoke.

"I'm not hoping for anything. I simply want to see what Goodwin had on his computer."

The fan in the computer continued to hum as my eyes stayed glued to the monitor. Suddenly there it was. The same capital letter 'I' showed up on the screen that appeared on Goodwin's monitor at home. Like the other computer, the letter stayed up only for one or two seconds then disappeared, replaced by the boot up sequence of the operating system. Like I said to Fred Martin, I'm no computer wizard, but I do know what is supposed to appear on a monitor when the computer is going through its boot up. I've never come across anything in any manual about the letter "I" appearing out of the blue. If it was on this computer and Goodwin's personal computer at home, that could only mean Goodwin put it there himself. That was not an impossible feat for a computer engineer.

In order to figure out why the letter "I" was showing up I was going to need the services of a computer geek of my own. It was obvious at this point I couldn't trust anyone at Cyber, so I was going to have to either bring my own computer whiz to the mountain or bring the mountain to my computer whiz. Since I was going to being spending a lot of time with this computer in the near future, I decided I didn't need to waste time looking at the hard drive now. I waited for the computer to finish loading the operating system, then began the shut down process. While the computer was going through its mechanizations, I swirled the chair to ask Sackett where I could find Mikah Johnston. He was gone. I guess he could take a hint.

I rose and walked out of the room. I worked my way back to the reception area, smiled at the same young girl still behind the desk and received a fake smile back (she was obviously a fast learner). From there it was a hop, skip and jump to Mikah Johnston's office. I entered through the double glass doors that separated Johnston's outer office reception areas from the hallway and walked up to the desk. Jenny St. Pierre looked up and smiled.

"Finished already with your investigation? I guess the really good detectives don't waste time."

I looked around the large elegantly appointed chamber, saw no one else in the room and decided to play Jenny's game.

"I don't waste time on the important things in life, like last night," I replied with a grin, sitting myself on the edge of the large walnut desk behind which Jenny was seated.

"I hope that doesn't mean you find our little matter of small importance in the grand scheme of things, Barry," came a voice from behind me. It was Mikah Johnston.

Jenny was turning scarlet and I winced. Slowly turning, I saw Mikah standing in the doorway to his private office, a slight smile playing on his lips.

"On the contrary," I said jumping from the desk to my feet. "I find it not only important, but fascinating as well. And the further I dig the more fascinating it becomes."

"Does that mean you already have something?" He became serious. "Come in and tell me." He stood aside to make room for me to pass into his office, then followed and closed the door. We crossed the room and sat, I in the large leather arm chair directly in front of the huge maple desk that dominated the room, Mikah in his chair behind the desk.

I didn't waste time. "I understand that it was you who pushed to hire Goodwin out of college."

Johnston seemed a little taken aback, but only momentarily. He simply shrugged. "That's right," he said. "It seemed like a win-win situation for the company. Larry was a local hero and a bright computer engineer. From a business standpoint, hiring him kept him out of the hands of our competitors. From a public relations standpoint, it was a real coup. Why do you ask?"

"Were you aware when you hired him that he had a gambling problem?"

The question shook Mikah; he sat up ramrod straight. "No, I did not. How did you find out?"

"His landlord. He's into a bookie for over one hundred thousand."

"What? Oh, shit!" He stood up and walked to the large window behind his desk overlooking the lake. He was quiet for a moment, and then he turned back towards me. "Do the police know?"

I nodded. "Fred Martin, my old partner, was with me when the landlord spilled the beans."

"Then we know tomorrow's headline: 'Cyber Employee Murdered; Links to Gamblers Found!' That's just great!"

"I wouldn't worry too much about it, Mikah."

He stared at me for a second. "Why not?"

"Because it will turn out to be a dead end. I already talked to the bookie in question. I'm willing to bet, no pun intended, that he was more surprised to hear Goodwin was dead than you were to find him this morning. It may actually turn out to be a small help to us."

"What do you mean?"

"You were right when you said the gambling link will be the heart of the headline in the papers. It makes tantalizing news when murder is mixed up with something else that's illegal, like gambling or drugs. The papers will want to know how the police are following up on the matter. And that means the police will have to spend time and manpower following up. That will keep them out of the real investigation."

"The real investigation?" Johnston echoed, his brow furrowed.

I stood up and walked around the desk to join Johnston. "Larry Goodwin was killed inside the plant. No bookie would ever be able to get into this place unseen or uninvited, and Goodwin certainly wasn't about to invite Vinnie in."

"Vinnie? Who's Vinnie?"

"Vinnie Lombardi, the bookie Goodwin owed the money to. We had a little chat a while ago. Goodwin has spent a lot of his free time doing everything he could to keep away from Vinnie. That means whoever killed Goodwin either works in the company or has access to the plant."

"We already figured that out this morning," said Johnston.

"Which brings me to my investigation as of this moment. I need Goodwin's computer."

"His computer? You mean the one in his office?"

"That's right."

Mikah Johnston turned away from me and walked to the other side of the room, sitting on the plush sofa situated on the wall opposite the window.

"I don't know if I can do that, Barry," he said.

"Why not?"

"Remember this morning I told you that we're in the process of negotiating some sensitive deals with some government agencies, both city and state?"

"I remember. But what has that…?"

"Goodwin was working on most of those contracts. He has all the details locked up in his computer. If I let that computer out of this plant and the information gets out, Cyber Inc. is dead in the water as a viable company. I'm afraid I just can't do it."

"Alright then, how about this. Let me bring in my own computer guy to dig into the computer. I'm not interested in the hard drive or the files on the drive. I'm only interested in the boot registry."

"The what?"

"The boot registry. There's something funny going on when his computer boots up."

"What's it doing?" asked Johnston.

After I explained, Johnston sat on the edge of the sofa staring at me.

"That's it? That's why you want me to open up the computer to you and whoever else with all those files in it?"

"You should know that the same thing is happening with Goodwin's personal computer at his home. And the police not only know about it, they have that computer."

"I don't care about that computer," said Johnston, raising his voice. He stood up and moved over to the desk. "Goodwin didn't have any company files on his personal computer. He wasn't allowed to take any information out of the plant."

"He also wasn't supposed to gamble, but he did," I said. "And he wasn't supposed to get killed, but he did that, too." Johnston and I were beginning to get in a very animated discussion. I saw it and switched gears, lowering my voice and resting my hands on the desk. "Look, Mikah, I don't know how long it will be before the police look into Goodwin's computer, if ever. I'm not interested in the files he has on the hard drive. All I want to do is bring in a computer wizard to check out the boot registry."

"Why can't we use somebody from the company? Why does it have to be an outsider?"

"Who are we going to trust?"

Johnston thought for a second, and then nodded his head. "Okay, have it your way. But I want to be there when you check out the computer."

"No problem," I smiled, straightening up. I walked around the desk and headed for the door.

"By the way," asked Johnston, "whom are you bringing in to open the computer?"

"I'm not sure," I answered, opening the door and turning back to look at him. "I have to see if the man I want is out of jail yet."

Chapter 6

I left Cyber Inc. and drove down East Street. It was 2:30 p.m. and I had a couple of administrative tasks to handle. The first was a trip to the mayor's office. Just as I reached Park Square I turned right onto Allen Street, then right again onto Fenn Street and miraculously found a parking spot close to City Hall. The city hall building of Pittsfield is a beautiful columned artifice that once housed the post office. Then the federal government in its infinite wisdom recognized that it needed a much more ugly one-story abode. The city raced in, grabbed the old post office and set up shop. Our mayor's office, like most mayors' offices around this country, was in the corner on the second floor.

I entered the building through the Fenn Street entrance and took the stairs two at a time. I walked into the reception area and stood in front of a desk at which was seated Molly Reagan, the mayor's administrative assistant. Molly's head was down as she was scanning some papers, but that didn't stop her from saying, "Hi, Barry. What took you so long? The mayor has been expecting you for the past two hours." She looked up and smiled at me.

"I'm a busy man, Molly." I smiled back. "Places to go, people to see. You can't expect me to drop everything just because some hot shot politician wants to see me."

"'Hot shot politician,' huh?" said Molly. "Just get your sorry butt into his office. I have to hold a bunch of important phone calls just so you and he can shoot the breeze, so make it fast."

"Yes, ma'am," I said, the smile still on my face. I turned and headed for the private office behind and to the left of her desk. Molly Reagan was the cog that made City Hall work efficiently. I knew it wasn't the mayor who was giving me ten minutes or so of his time, it was Molly.

I approached the oak door with the words "Mayor's Office" in gold embossed writing on it. I noticed the letters "I" and "E" were fading into obscurity and I was momentarily tempted to wipe out the "C" as well. But then, Marcus never did have much of sense of humor when it came to practical jokes, so I simply gave the door a perfunctory knock, opened it and walked through.

"Hello, Barry." Marcus Thomasson smiled, rising from behind a huge oak desk. "I've been expecting you." He came up to me, shook my hand and then gestured toward a couple of easy chairs. I took his cue and seated myself.

"Sorry, Marcus," I said, "but I've had a somewhat busy morning."

"So I hear. So, how's the investigation coming?"

The mayor knew my client was Cyber Inc., and as such giving him any information would be a breach of confidentiality on my part. But he also knew I would give him only those facts he could probably get from Sarcovich, only he would get them faster and in a less formal way from me.

Marcus Thomasson and I were old friends. We had met when we were both assigned to Camp Pendleton in California. I was an MP and Marcus was a Navy lawyer assigned to the JAG outfit. Our first meeting was less than auspicious. He was walking back from a restaurant when a trio of local toughs thought it would be fun to hassle a uniform. Had there only been one or two assailants Marcus would have been okay; he's pretty tough for a lawyer. The third guy swung the difference in their favor, which is when I showed up. Needless to say we made quick work of them, hauled their tails off to jail and then struck up a friendship. As it turned out, Marcus was from Pittsfield, born and bred.

Our friendship grew as time went by, and we were pretty tight by the time Marcus was discharged, six months before I was. He returned to Pittsfield, and using all the friends he had in town in the legal profession and in city politics managed to snag a spot for me on the police force when my discharge papers came through. Yep, he's the one I told you about. He's the one responsible for me being where I am today. That's why I give him so much grief; if not for Marcus, I would never have met Sarcovich, and my life would be much happier. Several minutes later I was finished giving the mayor some of the facts I had spent the day gathering.

"Goodwin was a gambler, huh?" remarked Marcus, rubbing the back of his neck. "That won't play well for Mikah Johnston when the papers get hold of the information."

"Guess not," I said in a noncommittal tone. I had no trouble filling Thomasson in on the gambling aspects of the case since they were definitely going to come out anyway. But I wasn't going to spoonfeed him the implications of all those facts. He would eventually figure out the gambling issue was a dead horse, probably even before the media did. But in the meantime, I was content to let him focus on it.

There was a knock on the door, immediately followed by Molly Reagan's head popping into the room. "Sorry to break up this little chit-chat, Marcus, but Melissa Randall is outside," she said.

"That's fine, Molly. Barry and I are done. Send her in."

I took that as my cue and rose to my feet. "I'll be at Jake's around four if you want me, Marcus."

"That sounds good," smiled the mayor. "I can use it as an excuse to pop in for a quick one."

We got about halfway to the door when it opened once more and Assistant Mayor Melissa Randall walked in. She saw us and stopped suddenly.

"Oh, I'm sorry. I thought you were free, Marcus. Molly told me to…"

"That's perfectly okay, Melissa," said Thomasson. "I believe you know Barry Dunleavy."

"Not well," she replied. "We've met once or twice in passing, Mr. Dunleavy; when you were on the police force."

"I remember," I replied. I would have had to be brain dead not to remember. Melissa Randall was one of the most beautiful women I had ever met, or seen for that matter. She was young, only in her mid-thirties I would guess. She was tall, long-legged, with striking red hair. Her meteoric rise in Pittsfield politics was due to her intelligence, family connections, and, not least of all, her own ambition. She was well liked and well respected (not an easy thing in Pittsfield political circles). And were it not for Marcus Thomasson's atmospheric popularity among the voters of the city, Melissa Randall would almost certainly be in the corner office.

Randall stuck out her hand and I took it. I received a handshake that would have made a three-hundred-pound wrestler wince. I tried to give her back an equally strong squeeze but I'm sure I fell woefully short.

"I'll see you sometime again, Marcus," I said, turning to the mayor so as to hide the fact that I was rubbing my right hand and feeling for broken bones.

"Right, Barry," answered Thomasson. "I'll be in touch."

I turned back toward the door, gave Melissa Randall a short nod and walked out of the room. I looked at my watch. It was 3:10 p.m.; just enough time, I decided, to cross the street to police headquarters and see if my computer wizard was out on parole yet.

Less than three minutes later I was standing in the entrance hall of police headquarters. Although a nondescript building of offices and holding cells, it nonetheless brought back memories, some fond and some not-so fond. One thing was for certain, the smell of the place hadn't changed. I nodded to the officer manning the front desk behind the glass partition, an old acquaintance from my time on the force, and then headed for the stairs. Stopping at the second floor, I made a beeline for the detective's area. I pushed open the swinging doors and entered a large nondescript room with several desks scattered about, some empty and some manned. Fred was manning one in the far corner. He looked up and saw me. He nodded me over.

"You must have more guts than brains, Barry," he said as I sat down in the chair that was butted up against the side of his desk. "The chief is in his office. He could show up here at any moment."

"I know," I answered, "but I need some information, and it's the kind I can only get out of a police file."

"So I'm supposed to put my butt on the line for you?"

"For me and the beer I'm going to buy you at Jake's later on." I smiled.

"Two beers," corrected Fred. "Don't forget the little lie this morning about going to North Adams. That's going to cost you."

"How did you know about my trip to see Lombardi?" I asked.

"I didn't," grinned Fred, "but you just admitted it. Now you owe me three beers, one for being so easily tricked."

"Oh well, that will teach me never to trust a cop. Now, how about that help?"

"What do you need?"

"Check the file on Mario DeRigger. See if he's out of jail yet?"

"DeRigger? You mean the guy you sent up just before you left the force? The heroin addict?"

"That's the guy," I agreed. "He went up for seven years, but I think he might be eligible for parole. If he was a good boy in jail, he may have hit the streets already."

Fred turned towards his computer and hit a few keys. It took a little bit longer than it should have because Fred had to keep checking a sheet with the different computer codes listed on it; in addition to not knowing much about computers he was a slow typist. Eventually the correct screen popped up.

"Here we go," muttered Fred. "DeRigger, Mario. Sentenced: seven years, Heroin, possession with intent to distribute; Arresting Officer: Barry Dunleavy, Lieutenant, Pittsfield Police Force; Paroled... Well what do you know?" Fred turned to me and smiled. "Last week!"

"And since his old man in Worcester disowned him after his arrest," I said, "he has nowhere to go but..."

"Right back here," Fred finished the sentence for me. "Let me check for an address." My old partner turned back to the computer, checked a few more codes on the sheet and punched them in. "Here we are: 73 Curtis Street." Turning back to me, he asked, "So why do you need to know...?"

"Dunleavy!"

One of the few secrets to life I have managed to discover in my short time on this planet is that timing is everything. It doesn't matter how smart you are, or think you are; it doesn't matter how lucky you are, although luck is usually better than brains; what really counts is being in the right place at the right time. For once in my life, my timing was perfect. I had gotten all the information I needed and now I was not going to have to explain to Fred Martin why I needed it. All thanks to Sarcovich. I stood up and turned to face the doors I had entered through. As I did so, I heard Fred hit a key on the computer keyboard. Without looking, I knew it was the delete key; he had wiped the screen clear of DeRigger's file.

"Hello, Chief." I smiled.

"I told you this morning to stay away from here. Unlike you, we're not the paid lapdogs of Cyber!"

"First of all, the correct phrase is 'highly paid lapdog.' Secondly, I'm here as a concerned citizen providing information to the police, not as a private investigator trying to get information."

Sarcovich scowled, looked toward Fred and then back to me. "What the hell are you talking about?"

It was time for the Big Lie, the one I had prepared for just such a contingency as coming face-to-face with Sarcovich in his own police station. "As I was driving down North Street, I thought I saw a man I had arrested several years ago for burglary hanging around DeLineo's Jewelers. I wasn't certain if it was the same man, so I came here and told Fred. He was just checking to see if the man I arrested was still in jail or was out yet. He's still in, so I was mistaken. Oh well, better safe than sorry."

Sarcovich looked at me for a second, and I could tell he was wrestling with my statement. It sounded like a plausible story, but it was coming from me and that made it hard for the chief to swallow.

He walked past me and looked at Fred Martin's computer screen. "Why is it blank?" he asked.

""Uh, we were done checking on the man, Chief..." began Fred.

"...So there was no sense in keeping the information up," I finished.

Sarcovich stared at me for a good five seconds, then he turned back to Fred. "Bring it back up."

Okay, so my plan wasn't foolproof. I hadn't counted on the chief to check out my story. Based on our past history, he would simply bellow some threat and then kick me out of the building. I made a mental note to more carefully think through my plans in the future. For the moment, however, I simply stared at my former partner. Fred sat staring at the computer monitor with pursed lips, obviously thinking about what he should do. If he called up DeRigger's file, Sarcovich would see he had nothing to do with burglary and know I was lying. After a second, Fred began to punch in something on the keyboard.

The chief reached into his breast pocket, pulled out a pair of reading glasses, put them onto the end of his nose, stared at the screen and began reading aloud, "Martin 'Marty' Fleiss; Arrested: burglary, still incarcerated." Sarcovich looked up at me and said, "Okay, Dunleavy. You did your duty. Thanks and get out."

I nodded to Sarcovich, allowed myself a small grin and turned toward the door. As I walked through the detective's room I congratulated myself on my lying ability. Granted, Fred played a role in the ploy by calling up the name of a man he and I had arrested eight years earlier for a string of burglaries in the area. That was another one I owed my former partner.

He was obviously thinking the same thing because as I reached the door Fred called out, "Four!"

It was just after 4 p.m. and finally time for Jake's. I didn't have to worry about fighting rush hour traffic since the police station is a short block from the Park Square Circle and Jake's is on the circle. Unfortunately, it's on the opposite side of the circle from the station. Rather than drive through Dead Man's Curve at, as I said, rush hour, an act somewhat akin to dressing like a mallard, jumping into a lake and quacking, all during hunting season, I took the coward's way out and walked. Fortunately, Pittsfield has a law that drivers must stop for pedestrians in cross walks, no matter what the traffic light says. Therefore, when I reached East Street, I waited for what seemed an eternity for the light to change, looked both ways six times and then ran like hell. I made it to the far sidewalk and, resisting the urge to drop to my knees and kiss the cement, headed three doors down to Jake's Tavern.

A few words about Jake's. It is not a bar. Bars are dark and smell of dried beer and are filled with smoke. Jake's has huge windows in the front letting in more light than any self-respecting drunk can handle, and that's not counting the glow from the six television screens scattered around the place. Secondly, while Jake's offers about one hundred different types of beer, ninety-nine of which you never heard of and ninety-five of which you would have to be totally drunk to even think of trying. Any scent of dried beer is totally overcome by the smell of enchiladas, refried beans and salsa from the Mexican hors d'ouvres modern "taverns" like to serve. As for the smoke, Pittsfield requires establishments like this one to set off designated spots for smokers to partake of their sport, and it's up to the owner to pick the spot. Jake, having watched his old man die a lingering and painful death from lung cancer, designated the dumpster out back of the tavern, and then only if you're standing in said dumpster. If you feel like smoking and don't know where the dumpster is, the twenty or so off-duty cops at the bar will be more than happy to show you where it is.

As I passed through the door I was met by the usual sight: many of the city's bigwig attorneys, seated at their "private" tables by the front window. Jake was no dummy. When it came time for him to open his establishment he asked himself two questions: who are the biggest drinkers in town and how close could he get to their place of work? The answer to the first question was obvious: lawyers and cops. The second answer was equally obvious: on the circle, one block from the police station and two doors down from the courthouse.

He had a built-in lunch and happy hour crowd. By jazzing his menu up a little and strategically placing his TVs around the room, not to mention keeping the boys in blue happy enough to hang around a little longer than necessary, he made the place bright and cheery enough, not to mention safe enough, for couples and families to come out for dinner.

But right now it was too early for dinner. The cops would be filing in for happy hour any time now, and the lawyers were already happy, especially the ones who had their cases dismissed three hours earlier. A few of them gave me a smile and a nod as I passed by on my way to the bar. Standing behind the bar talking to one of the customers was Alicia Dougherty, Jake's girlfriend and a high school pal of Jenny's. She saw me seat myself on a stool and walked over.

"Barry, long time no see," she smiled as she placed a cocktail napkin and a bowl of peanuts in front of me.

"I was just in here last night, Alicia," I said, reaching for the nuts.

"For you, that's a long time. What would you like?"

"I'll have a Sam Adams." I slid my head a little to the left and looked through the door leading to the kitchen. "Jake around?"

"You just missed him," she answered, filling my glass from the tap. "He had to make a bank run; we're short on ones and fives. It's those damn lawyers," and she nodded her head in the direction of the bar association meeting taking place at the tables in the far corner. "Order the cheapest beer in the place and never have anything smaller than a fifty. Just once I'd like to hear somebody say 'keep the change.'"

I had followed Alicia's eyes to the lawyers, now I turned back to her. "Well, you won't hear it from that crowd. They'll call you on the phone and tell you they'll take your case for free, then send you a bill for the phone call."

She smiled. "No one knows that better than me, Barry." She turned back to the customer she had left to serve me, stopped and then said, "Hey, Barry. Looks like there's going to be a town meeting."

I looked at her and followed her eyes again, this time toward the front door. Walking in were Marcus Thomasson, Fred Martin and Wally Cherski, the District Attorney. Cherski was an old drinking buddy of mine. He had been on the force when I joined, but he was on his way out. Wally was smart, too smart to stay a cop very long. He had gone to school and earned his law degree. He had actually been offered the job of police chief, but since he was only one course away from graduating law school he turned it down. A good cop, good lawyer, good DA.

"Look at this," I said after they spotted me at the bar (not hard since I was in my usual spot). "If it isn't the Three Stoo—Musketeers!"

"Very funny, Barry." Wally smiled as he walked around me and gave my neck a playful squeeze with his two very large hands. He sat down and grabbed a handful of nuts from the bowl in front of me. "So how have you been? I haven't seen you in about a month."

I nodded. "Yep, last time was when I single-handedly helped send Marchessi up for drug dealing."

"Yeah," agreed Wally. "You and the state police and the Massachusetts Drug Task Force and the city cops and..."

"Okay, okay. By the way, where's that dinner you promised to buy me when Marchessi was convicted?"

"All in good time, Barry. I don't want it to look like I bribed you to give testimony against the guy."

I turned and looked at Marcus Thomasson who was standing on my left, and asked him, "Is he kidding?" Marcus was waiting for his martini. It was known all over town that all Marcus ever drank were martinis, so when he came in Alicia made one for him without waiting for his order. The drink came and he sipped it.

"Oh, Alicia, you are an angel. It's been a rough day and you make the best martini in town." He put the glass down on the bar, turned to me and said, "Of course he's kidding. Wally's the cheapest bastard in the county, you know that. He's waiting until you forget he owes you dinner."

I turned back to Wally, who was sipping a beer. I hadn't heard him order one, and then I looked down at the bar and noticed my glass was gone. I said to Marcus, "You're right; he is a cheap bastard."

"Alright, enough of this chit chat." It was Fred, and if anyone in the room had a rough day, it was Fred. He had ordered his drink, already had it in his hand and was getting ready to order the second round. "Why don't you three guys go find us a table? I'll order Wally a beer, get the next round set up and meet you there?" I could see Fred was definitely ready for happy hour.

A couple of lawyers at a table on the back wall looked our way, gave Wally a disgusted look, stood up and walked out. There aren't many good things you can say about people not liking you, but at least you never have to worry about a crowded room.

Did I mention Wally Cherski was the most honest man I had ever met? When the lawyers who had just vacated their table were defending a suspected rapist, their defense included some not very nice and not very ethical actions toward the victim. Wally was all over them like a crow on road kill. He had them in front of the ethics committee and nearly had them disbarred. My friend may not have been the most well liked man in judicial circles in Berkshire County, but everyone knew who the top dog was and what his rules were.

We sat down at the newly vacated table and before we were settled in were joined by Fred. He was holding a tray with four glasses of beer and a martini.

"You expecting the city council to join us, Fred?" asked Marcus glancing at the tray.

"One beer is my first," explained the cop as he placed the tray in the middle of the table and sat down. "The other three beers and the martini are the second round. I knew you guys wouldn't want to wait."

"That's very considerate of you," I said.

"Actually, it's considerate of you; I put it on your tab." Fred simply looked at me and shrugged. "Hey, I told you back at the station that you owed me four beers; now we're even."

"Friends," I said, smiling at the three men at my table. "I'm surrounded by friends."

"And you're lucky to have us," said Wally, downing the last half of his (my!) beer and grabbing his second round off the tray. "Fred's filled me in on his investigation of the murder at Cyber; how's your end coming?"

"I spent the day following leads into the background of the victim," I replied. Telling Marcus all the details of the investigation was one thing, but I could never let Wally know what was going on at Cyber; I knew he would have to use any inside information I gave him in a trial. I could give him the barest outline and that would make him happy. What's more, he knew that was all he was going to get from me. However, that didn't stop me from talking about what the police already knew. "Besides," I continued, "I still think that computer we found in Goodwin's apartment this morning may hold some key information."

"What computer is that?" asked Wally.

Fred jumped in. "Barry and I found some high-tech and pricey computer equipment in Goodwin's place this morning. A laptop comes up with some strange message on boot up. Barry thinks there's something to it. I brought all the computer equipment to the station and checked it in to the Property room. Harry Prouty, our computer guy, will check out the laptop tomorrow when he gets back from vacation."

"Do you think it has anything to do with the victim's death?"

"Beats me," replied Fred. "But then again, that's what I'm hoping to find out from Harry."

"Excuse me for interrupting, gentlemen," came a voice from behind us. We all turned in our chairs to see Melissa Randal standing there in all her Amazonian beauty. There was a race between the four men at our table to see who would get up first and appear the more mannerly. I lost, thanks to Wally using my shoulder as leverage to heave his two-hundred-and-fifty-pound bulk up. But since he came in second to Marcus, I didn't make a big deal about it.

"Hello, Melissa," gurgled the district attorney, forgetting that he had a mouthful of beer. It's sad to see what a beautiful woman can do to an otherwise intelligent man. Fortunately I'm not very intelligent, so I get to make a fool of myself with no recriminations; at least, that's what Jenny tells me. I therefore rose to my feet and offered Melissa Randall a free chair.

"Thanks, Barry," she cooed. Okay, maybe "cooed" wasn't the

right word, but a man can dream. "I just came looking for Marcus." She turned to the mayor and continued, "You forgot to sign these papers and we need to present them to the city council at the meeting tonight."

She reached into her briefcase and pulled out a manila folder. As Marcus, but not the rest of us, sat down, Randall placed the folder on the table in front of him, opened it and handed the mayor a pen. As he signed the various papers, she straightened up and smiled at the rest of us.

"Boy's night out and you didn't invite me?" Still no cooing, but this time with a definite softening in the voice.

"Melissa, you know you have a standing invitation to join us anytime," replied Wally. It was like watching a bull elephant trying to court a nightingale; not a pretty sight.

"Thanks, Wally. That's nice of you. But right now," she continued as she bent over once more to close the folder and remove it from the table, "I have to get these papers back to City Hall and ready for tonight's meeting. However, I will keep it in mind for future reference. Goodbye, gentleman." She turned and walked out of Jake's Tavern, everyone but Marcus following her with our eyes until she was safely across the circle and headed back down Allen Street.

It was Fred who came back to life first. "I don't know how you do it, Marcus."

"Do what?" asked the mayor, slowly sipping his second martini.

"Work with that woman all day long and still keep your mind on business."

"That's not a problem," he snorted. "She's not interested in men."

It took Marcus a few seconds to realize the three of us were staring at the man with open mouths. He looked at us for another second or two before he realized what we were thinking. He started to laugh.

"She's not interested in women either." He took another sip of his drink. "At this stage in her life, she's not interested in anything but her work. She comes in early and goes home late; works weekends, holidays and everything in between. She doesn't have time, or the inclination, for someone to share her life."

"Speaking of sharing a life, Barry," smiled Wally as continued to look out the window. "Look who's coming."

I followed Wally's gaze and saw Jenny St. Pierre step out of the car she had just finish parking in front of the tavern.

Chapter 7

The day had started out with me getting the call to investigate one murder; it ended with me almost becoming the victim in a second. Before that, however, if you had come up to me in Jake's and asked how everything was going, I would have smiled, said fine, invite you to have a seat and join me in a drink. As a matter of fact, that's exactly what I did when Jenny sidled up to our table.

This time when I offered a beautiful woman a seat it was accepted. Jenny gently dropped into the chair, smiled at me and promptly turned her back and struck up a conversation with Fred. She does this to me all the time. If I said I was used to it I would be lying. If I said I understood why she did it, it would be an even bigger lie. The only time Jenny gives me her undivided attention is when we are alone, and while I know that sounds stupid ("If you're alone with her, who else is she going to pay attention to?"), let it be known that there have been times I've been alone with a woman and she didn't pay any attention to me at all.

Two could play this game, I said to myself as I looked around to find someone whom I could use to ignore Jenny. The mayor was at the bar trying to attract Martha's attention so our table could begin work on round three; Wally had gravitated to another table where he had spotted a couple of off-duty cops, one of whom was a witness in an upcoming trial. That's when I noticed Sammy Brackens, the young officer I had met earlier in the morning on the way to Cyber. He had just entered the room and was working his way through the ever-enlarging crowd toward the bar. I caught his eye and motioned to an empty table on the other side of the room. He smiled and nodded, but continued his journey to the bar. I got up without a word to Jenny and Fred, still deep in conversation, and elbowed my way through the crowd. I passed Marcus on the way, grabbed my beer off his tray, mumbled a thanks and managed to grab the open table just before a couple of lawyers got their mitts on it. Sammy joined me about five minutes later, just as I was finishing my beer. He handed me one of the two he was carrying.

"How ya doin', Lieutenant?" he said as he sat and sipped at the same time.

"Thanks," I said, accepting the beer. "Pretty good, Sammy," I answered after a slow pull on the draft. "An interesting day, you might say."

I figured on killing two birds with one stone. First, I had to fill in Sammy, and through him the rest of the police force, on the murder investigation, or at least as much as I felt they should know. Secondly, I wanted to show Jenny that I could ignore her as much as she ignored me. I glanced over to the table I had just left and saw that Jenny was doing a much better job at it than I was. I turned back to Sammy.

"So I hear some guy at Cyber by the name of Goodwin was killed," said Brackens, trying to pick up the conversation from where it never got started earlier that morning.

"Yeah," I nodded. "Larry Goodwin, former All-American football player Cyber hired a while back as a software engineer."

"That's right too," said Sammy nodding. "I heard he was around here. Should have known he was working for Cyber if he was in town."

"Why do you say that?"

"Oh, the guys on different beats would mention seeing him here and there. You know, driving around in his flashy car, beautiful women in the car, that sort of thing."

Sammy sipped his beer, looked around the bar and continued with his thought, "The only beautiful woman in this bar is sitting over there with Detective Martin. Man, she's a looker."

I grunted my best assertive grunt, not bothering to look up from my beer; I knew he was talking about Jenny. Suddenly, however, a small bell went off in the back of my head.

"Hey, Sammy. Did you just say that some of the boys would see Goodwin driving around town in a flashy car?"

"Yeah, Lieutenant," he said, turning back towards me and gulping down the last of his beer. "Small, red sports car, don't remember the type. From the description, though, it was low slung, high priced and brand new."

That did not describe the piece of junk hauled from Goodwin's driveway this morning. And since his apartment house did not have a garage attached, that left the question: just where was this fancy red sports car. Or did it?

"When did the other cops say they last saw Goodwin's car?" I asked.

That brought Sammy's head up. He was young and inexperienced, but you could tell he had good police sense. He knew when he hit a vein that might hold gold, and now he knew to keep the conversation going in the right direction.

"Well, let's see. The last time anyone mentioned seeing Goodwin was...oh, must have been about two or three weeks ago. It was Phil Morrissey who saw him."

"Where did he see him?"

"Said it was over on South Street heading toward Lenox. I remember because Phil said he was doing about fifty-five in a thirty mile-per-hour zone."

"Did Morrissey stop him and ticket him?" I asked.

"Nah, Phil was answering a call and going the opposite way. Besides, he said Goodwin was just about at the city line. It was Lenox's headache."

"Was there anybody with Goodwin?"

"Phil said there was this drop dead gorgeous black-haired babe running her hands through his hair. Say, Lieutenant, I can tell this is important. Want to fill me in on why?"

"I'm trying to track down everyone who came into contact with Goodwin recently. Tell you what, Sammy. You give me some more good stuff and I'll keep you filled in on the investigation." It was a small lie and Sammy knew it. I wasn't going to spill all the beans to him or anyone else connected with the city. However, he knew that whatever he got out of me, coupled with what spilled out of the police station's detective division, would keep the boys in blue suits happy and feeling like they had an inside tract. Lies work best when everyone involved knows you're lying.

Sammy smiled. "Sure thing, Lieutenant. I hear anymore about Goodwin and you'll be the first to know."

"Let's drink on it," I said. "And this round's on me."

It was 8 p.m. and something in the back of my mind told me I needed to find that red sports car of Goodwin's. Jenny, on the other hand, was telling me that I needed to find a cop. And she may have been right. After all, someone had just fired a shot at me and missed by only a few inches.

By the time Sammy Brackens and I had finished our little meeting and I was returning to my original table, Jenny and Fred Martin were still in a little tête-à-tête. Fred saw me elbowing my way through the crowd and nodded to Jenny. I told you I was a detective and I notice these things.

"Oh, Fred," Jenny gurgled like a teenage schoolgirl as I approached the table. "You are so funny. I just wish other people were as funny as you."

"They are," I said, grabbing a chair, placing it between Fred and Jenny and sitting down. "It's just that they're dead and so not many people hear their jokes."

"Funny, Barry," smiled Fred. "Well, now that you're here to sweep up my remains, I guess I'll be on my way." He stood up and finished his beer in one gulp. "Try not to bore the lady too much, will you? Jenny, it was a pleasure and we'll have to do it again some time." He turned and started to leave.

"Try it," I called after him, "and I'll tell your wife." Fred responded with an ungentlemanly gesture and Jenny laughed.

"You forget that I know Fred's not married and never has been." Jenny smiled. "Now, are you ready to buy me dinner?"

"Just like that?" I asked, feigning indignation. "No 'Hello, Barry! How are you? Long time no see!'"

"I saw you this afternoon. And this morning. And last night. And now I'm hungry and want to know if you are going to take me to dinner like you promised."

"When did I promise to take you to dinner?" I protested.

"This morning!"

"I don't remember...."

"Early this morning!"

"Oh," I said, "now I remember." And I did, although I could be forgiven my lapse of memory given the timing of my promise. I made a mental note not to make promises in the middle of certain situations. "Where would you like to eat?"

Jenny stood up and grabbed her coat. "Mikal's, that new Greek restaurant on West Housatonic."

"You mean the one just a few blocks from my house?"

She turned to me and purred, "That's the one."

I had a dilemma. My car was parked about two blocks away in front of City Hall. Should I walk across Park Square, a little safer now that rush hour had passed, but still early enough for the drunks to still be in the bars; or should I let the car sit in front of the municipal building for the night and simply hitch a ride with Jenny?

"You may need your car some time between now and early tomorrow," replied Jenny after I repeated my question about cars aloud. "I'll drive you over to it. Hop in."

Now you may think I'm extremely lazy, not bothering to walk a few short blocks to my car. But you have not seen Jenny's wheels. A Porsche Boxster S: a two-door, forest green convertible with a six speed manual transmission.

"I'll drive," I volunteered as I angled my way to the driver's side of the vehicle.

"Sure," smiled Jenny, holding out her keys. I reached for them, but she quickly pulled back her hand. "You can drive your car just as soon as I drop you off at City Hall." She quickly jumped behind the wheel and gave me one of her sly smiles. I trumped her with one of my better moping frowns and slowly trudged around to the passenger side.

Jenny backed out of the diagonal parking spot in front of Jake's, rounded her way partially through the circle and shot onto Allen Street. Thirty seconds after hopping into the Boxster I was hopping into my own Toyota Corolla.

"Who leads?" called Jenny from her car.

"You! I always like looking at a pretty behind."

"Well, thank you, sir." She smiled back.

"I was talking about the Porsche. Now get going."

We shot up Fenn Street, hung an illegal left onto North and in a few moments were driving down West Housatonic. West Housatonic Street is actually Route 20 and if you follow it for about ten minutes you find yourself in New York State. Personally, I try never to go that far. I did manage to make it far enough to reach Mikal's, however. I followed as Jenny pulled into the gravel parking lot and was able to pull in only two cars down from her spot.

I got out and turned to walk over to her when it happened. The glass on the driver's side of my car shattered and then I heard the shot. Without hesitating, or ducking, I ran over to Jenny and threw her down on the ground between her car and another parked next to hers. Her muffled protests notwithstanding, I covered her body with mine. Hearing the squeal of tires on the road, I carefully raised my head. Roaring away from my field of vision was a dark blue late model Honda. I could make out two figures in the car, but that was about it.

"Are you planning on letting me up or should I just order take-out from the restaurant?"

I looked down at Jenny. Her hair was all mussed and she was smiling, but the tone of her voice told me the joke was more for her own benefit than mine; she was scared. I quickly helped her up, knocking away some of the gravel that had clung to her clothes.

"Who was that?" she asked almost nonchalantly, trying to show that her nerves were just as steely as mine.

"I have no idea," I replied still looking down West Housatonic Street in the opposite direction from which we had come. Then, turning back to Jenny, I asked, "Do you have your cell phone?"

"Of course. Should I call the police?"

"That would be a good idea, but don't ask for Fred. He already warned me once today that I could get hurt asking the wrong people questions. I really hate it when he's right."

"Is that what this is all about?" she asked while dialing 911.

"I don't know," I answered truthfully as I walked back to my car to inspect the damage. I looked through the broken window and immediately saw the bullet hole in the passenger door. *Good*, I thought, *it should be easy to trace the gun.*

Turning back toward Jenny, I said, "But if this does have something to do with it, I'm glad."

"Glad you got shot at?" Jenny asked shutting off her phone and returning it to her purse. She had reported the shooting while I was checking out my car.

"No, just glad I asked the right questions. It made them either angry or nervous."

"You know, Barry," said Jenny walking over to me, "you're the only person I know who, in less than one day, can piss somebody off enough to want to shoot you."

"It's a talent, my dear," I replied, bending down to kiss her cheek. "And it's all mine."

Dinner was not served. Or, to be more accurate, it was not served at the restaurant. By the time I was finished filling out the reports the police needed to go out and not find my two shooters, Mikal's was closed. But behind every cloud, as they say.

"Why don't we just go to your place and I'll make us something," Jenny offered between two large yawns.

"Sounds good," I answered, leading her by the arm toward her car. Mine was being impounded for the night so the police could go over it with a fine-tooth comb. Except for the bullet lodged in the passenger door, however, I had no idea what they hoped to find. After all, the two guys in the Honda never got closer than thirty feet to my car.

"I'll drive," I said again, only this time I meant it. Jenny was still shaken from the evening's events, despite her outward show of calm. Besides, I was so calm I needed something like a steering wheel to keep my hands from shaking. I led Jenny to the passenger side, opened the door and watched her get in. I walked around to the driver's side, pushed the seat from its forward position as far back as it would go and climbed in.

"How can someone with such long legs keep the seat so far up?" I asked.

"Long legs, short arms," Jenny replied.

"A small price to pay," I smiled.

Chapter 8

I was up by seven the next morning but Jenny still beat me. She had left an hour earlier so she could run home, shower and get to work by seven. Mikah Johnston had a meeting scheduled with some clients of Cyber Inc.'s at nine and Jenny wanted to go in early to make sure everything was in order. That did, however, leave me with the small problem of no transportation. The phone rang as I was getting out of the shower.

"Hey, Buddy!" sang Fred's voice over the phone. "I heard you had a little fun last night."

"You'll have to be more specific," I replied. "Define 'fun.'" He could have been referring to one of two things: the shooting, which had been interesting; and Jenny coming over to my place to make dinner, which had been slightly more than interesting.

"They missed, didn't they?" said Fred. I could hear the "I told you so" tone in his voice. "Anyway, I heard you're without wheels."

"No problem, Fred. I just put in new batteries for my thumb."

"Sorry, but hitching is illegal in Massachusetts. I'll be over in about thirty minutes to pick you up."

"Thanks," I murmured as I sipped my coffee. "But you don't have to…"

"It's on my way. See you in thirty." With that the receiver went dead.

Fred's house was not on the way. I lived on the west side of town; he lived on Pomeroy Avenue, five minutes south of the police station. He was either being a real pal or there was some ulterior motive in his going out of his way to pick me up.

There was an ulterior motive. I knew it as soon as I opened the door to let Fred in. He crossed my threshold without so much as a "Good morning"; instead, I heard: "We've got trouble."

"'We' as in you and me or 'we' as in you and the rest of the police force?" I asked as he headed for my kitchen to pour himself a cup of coffee.

"The police," he replied. He got a clean cup from the cabinet above the coffee maker, filled it about halfway up and took a swig. "Damn," he said, "who taught you how to make coffee?"

"What's wrong with it?" I answered defensively. Personally, I thought my coffee was pretty good.

"Nothing," said Fred, turning back to the coffee maker and filling his cup. "It's loads better than the stuff we get at the station. What's your recipe?"

"Try using the grounds only once, not four times," I answered as I made my way over to the kitchen table and sat down.

"Yeah, that sounds like a good idea," he mumbled as he took the seat across from me.

"Now, what's this about 'trouble'?"

"You know how I was telling you at Jake's last night we were waiting for Harry Prouty to return from vacation to check out that computer we found in Goodwin's apartment?"

"Yeah," I answered. "Don't tell me Harry's run off with a beautiful native girl and is not coming back."

"Harry went on one of those archaeology vacations to the Galapagos Islands. The only natives there he could run off with are turtles and lizards."

"So what's the problem?"

"Harry showed up to work this morning about an hour ago. I filled him in on the Goodwin case and we went down to the Property room together to get the computer."

"And?"

"It wasn't there."

"The computer is missing?" I asked, almost choking on my coffee.

"No, the computer is not missing. I checked it into the Property room myself yesterday after leaving you at Goodwin's place. The book doesn't show anyone signing out the computer or even coming to check on it. Somebody stole it from police headquarters."

I let out a low whistle, leaned back in my chair and took a sip of my coffee. "Boy, do you have trouble."

Fred dropped me off at the police impound lot off East Street where they had taken my car the night before. According to him the police found nothing in the car except the spent bullet imbedded in the passenger door; go figure.

"Sarcovich is going to chew somebody a new asshole," I told Fred as I was getting out of the car at the impound lot. "Who was in charge of the Property room last night?"

"Phil Morrissey. Poor guy. He isn't the usual Property room clerk, Joe Phillips is. Phillips called in sick yesterday at the last minute. Morrissey was in the squad room at the time just finishing up his shift. He said he would pull a double if they needed him, so they used him. Now his butt is in a sling."

"That's too bad," I said as I got out of Fred's car and slammed the door. Then I bent down and poked my head through the open passenger side window. "But the fact that Morrissey was new to this assignment means he's not up on Property room protocol. Somebody could have gotten in without Morrissey having him or her sign the book. Or he could have walked out for a few minutes without locking the room. Have you asked him about it?"

"He got off duty just as I was coming on. Pete Jacobs was on the phone to him to come back to the station as I was leaving to get you. We'll see what he has to say. You headed to Cyber?"

"In a little while," I answered. "I have to go see an old friend first."

"Anyone I should know about?" Fred asked, cocking his left eyebrow a fraction of an inch.

"That depends on what he has to say to me," I smiled back. "But if he has something that helps with the case, you'll be the first person I call."

"But I shouldn't hold my breath waiting to hear from you, is that it?"

"Depends on how long you can hold it," I replied. "Thanks for the ride." With that, I turned and walked over to the lot attendant to sign for my car. I then drove about a block down East Street to a glass replacement garage, had them put in a new driver's side window and was soon on my way.

Mario DeRigger was no longer a heroin addict; jail had helped clean him up. Truth be told, he never was much of an addict. Mario was into drugs to make money. His father was some bigwig in a computer company out in Worcester. Growing up, Mario had the inside track on all the computer innovations at his old man's company, and he made the most of it; he was a computer genius. He was smart and he was rich, just a real bad combination in a young man. He got himself hooked on drugs—so much for the smart part. When his father found out, he disowned him—so much for the rich part.

Mario was nineteen and needed a way to pay for his habit. He found himself a job as courier on the New York City-to-Springfield-to-Worcester heroin route. He did pretty well, too, for about ten months. Then he got greedy. He tried to expand the route west from Springfield into Pittsfield. He lasted four months, and then I caught him. He did his time in Springfield, and now with no place to call home, he had come back to our fair city. The Morningside district, to be exact.

Morningside was both commercial and residential. The heart of the district is Tyler Street. North of Tyler Street it was all residential, nice houses in nice clean neighborhoods. The south side of Tyler was also residential, but less nice and a lot less clean, and on occasions saw some colorful folks like DeRigger move in. Tyler Street itself was commercial, housing a plethora of small businesses ranging from bakeries to gas stations to hardware stores. Further east the area turned industrial thanks to the gigantic Cyber Inc. plant that snaked its way along the periphery of the neighborhood streets. Seventy-three Curtis Street was my destination of record.

I quickly found what I was looking for, and it was pretty much what I had expected. It was an old house that had been made into three flats, and not too recently. I climbed the porch steps, found Mario's name on the downstairs flat's mailbox, and rang the doorbell. I checked my watch, saw it was a little after eight and promptly decided I was going to get no answer even if I kept ringing the bell. I used my fist on the door, banging away with all my might. After about thirty seconds my efforts were rewarded. The door flew open and Mario stood there, black hair all disheveled, a four- or five-day growth of beard hiding his face and his eyelids shut tight enough to let just a minimum of sunlight in.

"Stop with the pounding already, whoever the hell you...Oh Christ, Dunleavy! What the hell do you want?"

"It's nice to see you, too, Mario," I said as I pushed by him and entered the house.

I looked around and saw that the flat was what I had expected it to be. I was standing in a small front parlor, with a larger living room just past it. Beyond that was a small kitchen with a door off the left that probably led to a bathroom and a second door on the right that looked out into the backyard. To the right of the living room was an open door and I could see part of an unmade bed. The apartment smelled of stale beer.

"Staying clean, Mario?" I asked, not bothering to turn to face him.

"No, Dunleavy," Mario sneered back. "I've been stoned ever since I got out of jail. What the hell do you think? I've got no money to buy food, let alone drugs. And even if I had a lot of cash, drugs are for suckers. I found that out the hard way."

I turned and looked at him, his five-foot-eight-inch rail-thin frame covered in a cheap cotton robe. Even when Mario was dealing he wasn't a big user, and I could tell from looking at him he was sober. What he looked like was a former rich boy with no money and no idea how to make any now that drugs were out of his life. He was lost and he knew it.

"No money for food, huh? That's too bad." I walked over to the sofa and sat down. I figured I would take this slow enough to determine what buttons were the right ones to push with DeRigger.

"Yeah, life's a bitch," answered Mario crossing over to the other side of the living room and sitting in a torn easy chair. "So what do you want?"

"A little help," I answered.

"From me? You want help from a guy you sent to prison? You've got a lot of nerve."

"Just thought you might want to make a little money," I replied. "If I'm wrong, just tell me to leave."

DeRigger stared at me, obviously torn between telling me to go to hell and wondering just how much money I was talking about. He didn't tell me to leave, instead he said, "I heard you're not a cop anymore. So what kind of help are you looking for?"

"Computer help," I said. "You still know your way around them?"

Mario smiled and nodded. "Kept up in prison. You'd be surprised how much the state is willing to spend on computers trying to rehabilitate people like me."

"Are you rehabilitated?"

"Depends on how much money we're talking?"

"How's three hundred sound?"

Mario's smiled left his face. He had obviously been thinking in the twenty to fifty buck range. "It sounds good. You being straight with me, Dunleavy? What do I need to do for this money?"

"I need you to check out a computer and tell me why it keeps booting up with a weird message."

"What kind of message?"

I stood up. "I'll show you when we get there." I stared at Mario for a moment. It was obvious that in his present condition he would be the talk of Cyber Inc. after he showed up. "You have any better clothes?"

Mario smiled. "Yeah, I got all my old things. A girlfriend held them for me while I was away."

"Seven years is a long time. Hope they're not out of style."

He got up and turned toward the bedroom. "Good clothes never go out of style. And back then I bought only the best. Give me ten minutes." He stopped at the bedroom door and turned back toward me. "By the way, where we going?"

"Cyber Inc. Oh yeah," I added. "You're going to meet the CEO."

Mario frowned. "CEO, huh? In that case I better shower. Give me twenty minutes." He turned and walked into the bathroom

"Take twenty-five and shave," I called after him.

Less than 45 minutes later I was driving up to the security shack at the Cyber plant (for some reason Mario had decided to shave twice). The guard from the day before, Tim Jackson, walked out to greet me.

"How ya doin', Barry?" he asked as he came up to my car.

"Still kicking, Tim," I answered. I nodded toward the plant and asked, "The police here today?"

"Nope, not yet. Although we've been told they could show up anytime."

"Well, I know from experience they'll come at the most awkward times, so be ready. By the way, am I still on your 'revolving' list?"

"You are," said Tim, "but your friend isn't. I'm going to have to get his name."

"Mario DeRigger," I answered and spelled the last name for him when he looked like he was having trouble writing it down on his clipboard. "Mr. Johnston will be wanting to see both of us," I volunteered.

"You know the way," the guard smiled as he backed away from

the car and waved me on.

"Thanks," I replied as I shifted the car into drive and started to pull away. But I slammed on the brakes immediately. I had just thought of something.

"Say, Tim!" I called out the open car window.

Jackson, who had turned toward his shack, stopped and retraced his steps back to my car.

"Yeah, Barry?"

"You said yesterday that you came on duty at six a.m., is that right?"

"That's what I said."

"And you didn't see Goodwin come into the plant?"

"Nope."

"So he must have come in earlier."

Jackson furrowed his brow. "Must have," he said. Then he brightened up. "The log-in book from the night security guard would have his arrival time."

"Can you check it for me?" I asked.

"I would if I had it, Barry," Jackson shrugged. "But the log books get turned into the head of security after a twenty-four hour period. Check with him."

"What's his name?"

"Charlie McCarthy."

"You're kidding me?" I smiled. "Charlie McCarthy, as in the famous dummy?"

"Yep," Jackson smiled back. "But don't crack any jokes about his name when you talk to him; he's heard them all and doesn't like any of them."

"Thanks for the warning, Tim." I pulled away from the security shack and headed for the first open parking spot I could find. As I was pulling into the spot, Mario turned toward me.

"So you pulled me out of a nice warm bed to go talk to a dummy?"

"No, I pulled you out of a nice warm bed to make some money. I'll talk with the dummy."

"Sounds like a good deal to me."

We got out of the car, headed for the main plant entrance and in a few minutes were in Mikah Johnston's administrative suite. Jenny was at her desk as usual.

"Who's your friend?" she asked looking at DeRigger. He was wearing his best clothes, which, I'm sorry to say, were a lot nicer than mine.

"Name's Mario, babe," said DeRigger sitting down on the edge of Jenny's desk. "And what might yours be?"

Jenny gave me a quick glance, and then turned back to DeRigger. "My name is Ms. St. Pierre," she replied, emphasizing the "Ms," while standing up. "And if you don't get your butt off my desk the only person you'll be introducing yourself to is a doctor."

Jenny knew about DeRigger; we had discussed the possibility of my bringing him in to see Mikah over dinner the night before. Had that not been the case, Jenny's reaction would have been much more restrained and less, shall we say, crude. But Mario was unaware of that, so his reaction was one of shock, followed by a quick retreat to his feet. Jenny smiled at Mario and sat back down.

"Please have a seat, gentlemen," Jenny purred. "Mr. Johnston is in a meeting, but he will be with you shortly."

"She's tough," DeRigger said to me as we sat down on an oversized sofa, far enough from Jenny's desk so that she could not hear us.

"Tougher than you," I answered. "If I were you, I'd be on my best behavior around her. And Mikah Johnston," I added as an afterthought.

"He's a suit," sneered Mario. "Just like all the suits at my old man's company. I've been dealing with that kind for years."

"He may be a suit," I said, "but he's a suit with a brain. And he's even tougher than that young lady who just handed you your head."

"I can handle him."

I turned to DeRigger and put my hand on his shoulder. From Jenny's view of things, it looked like a simple touch, but Mario was beginning to wince from the pressure I was exerting.

"Let's get one thing straight, Mario," I said, keeping my hand firmly on his shoulder. "I work for Mikah Johnston and you work for me, at least at this moment. I need you to find out what's going on with a certain computer, and Johnston is the only person who can give us permission to look at the damn thing. If he says 'No, you can't touch the computer,' well, then I don't need you anymore. If I don't need your help, I don't need to pay you three hundred dollars. Therefore, you will be courteous and professional when you talk to him. Do I make myself clear?"

Mario was beginning to squirm under the pressure. "Yeah, I understand," he managed to get out under his breath. I let go of his shoulder.

"Good," I smiled. "I always like to have an understanding with the people I work with."

A few minutes later we were told Johnston was ready to see us. We left the sofa and entered his opulent office. From the look on Mario's face as he gazed around, I would say he was duly impressed. His father may have been an executive in a company, but not a company on the scale of Cyber Inc. After the introductions, I brought up the reason for our visit with Johnston.

"Mr. DeRigger is the man I was telling you about yesterday," I said. "He should be able to tell us what's going on with that computer of Goodwin's."

Johnston turned to look at Mario. "So tell me, Mr. DeRigger, is what Barry said yesterday true? Did you just get out of prison or was that just one of his little jokes?"

Mario looked at me, and if looks could kill I'd be laying on the floor stiffer than Larry Goodwin. It was obvious that Mario had been hoping to sweet talk his way with Johnston, but that was before he found out the CEO knew his background. He was now at a disadvantage, and that's exactly what I wanted.

Turning back to Johnston, Mario answered, "No joke, Mr. Johnston."

"What were you in for?"

"Drugs."

"Dealing or using?"

"A lot of the first, a little of the second."

"Still dealing?"

"No."

"Still using?"

"No."

Mikah turned to look at me. "Is he telling the truth?"

I shrugged. "As far as I know."

"Okay, let's go look at that computer." Without another word, Johnston stood up, walked around his desk and out his office door. I gave a nod to Mario, who, frowning, was still trying to figure out what had just happened, and we both stood up and followed.

"All right, here we are," said Mikah minutes later as we all stood in Goodwin's office. It wasn't easy, as the room was obviously meant for two people or less. "Do whatever it is you have to do, Mr. DeRigger."

Mario moved forward, shouldering his way past Mikah and I. He sat down at the desk in front of the computer and turned it on. We all watched the screen closely, waiting for the single capital letter 'I' to appear. On the way to Cyber, I had told Mario what to look for, but that was not what popped up on the screen. After the initial boot sequence was completed, suddenly not one, but two words appeared. The words 'WAS KILLED' flashed on the monitor for approximately two seconds then disappeared to be replaced by the remainder of the boot sequence.

Mario turned back to look at me. "That's not what you said was going to happen."

"That's not what happened yesterday," I answered.

"How is it possible for the computer to switch messages every day?" asked Mikah

"It's obvious what's going on," said Mario.

Mikah Johnston and I waited for him to finish his explanation, but nothing was forthcoming. After a few seconds, I asked. "And that would be…?"

"Since this computer belongs to a computer programmer who was killed, and the first two messages coming from the computer begin the sentence 'I was killed...' the man obviously has written a program to announce who bumped him off, and it adds to that message every so often."

"How often?" I asked.

"Did you see the same message two days ago?"

"No, Goodwin wasn't dead two days ago. What's that got to do with anything?"

"That message you saw with the letter "I" might have been on the boot up sequence for one, two or even ten days or more. Without knowing what the message said the day before Goodwin died I can't know what day the message changes."

"The program knows what day it is?" asked Mikah.

"Every computer has a built-in clock and calendar. The program this Goodwin guy wrote seems to be telling the computer that it should change the message every 24 hours, or 48 hours or longer. He could just as easily have had the message change once a week, once a month, or even once a year."

The obvious idea immediately struck me. "So change the clock in the computer to read tomorrow's date, then start the computer again and we'll see tomorrow's message."

"That wouldn't be the smartest thing in the world to do," answered DeRigger.

"Why not?" asked Mikah.

"Because we don't know what safeguards he's placed on the program."

"What do you mean 'safeguards'?"

Mario sighed lightly and smiled. "Okay, gentlemen. Here is your first and only course in Computers 101. When a computer is first powered up, the BIOS is the first thing executed by the system. The BIOS provides a basic set of instructions used to boot the computer. The BIOS performs all the tasks which need to be done at startup, including performing self-diagnostics and initializing the hardware in the computer."

"So what you're saying," I interrupted, "is that the BIOS is where the program Goodwin wrote is located."

"No, that's not what I'm saying. The program Goodwin wrote has a line of code telling the BIOS to run it on startup. The program could be anywhere on the computer."

"So where do these safeguards you mentioned come in?" I asked.

"If they exist," explained Mario, "they exist in the program itself. They, too, are lines of code. They could be anything that protects the computer program from being adjusted."

"Protect the program how?"

"In a lot of different ways. Goodwin could have told the program to erase itself if someone tried to change the computer's clock; he could have told the program to start from scratch if someone attempted to change the BIOS. He could have done any of a million things. The short version is that if I try to do something to make the program run out of synch, I could end up wiping the program out all together."

"Does that mean you can't do anything?" asked Mikah.

DeRigger looked at Johnston and myself with a Cheshire cat grin pasted on his face. "I never said I couldn't do what you want. I've yet to meet a computer program I can't handle. What I'm saying is that I need to proceed slowly. If I make a mistake by rushing blindly around this thing, there's no going back. Just give me a little time."

"Which means I have to leave you alone with this computer," said Johnston. "And that was something I didn't want to do. I have a full schedule today and I can't spend all my time watching over your shoulder."

"Don't you trust me?" smiled DeRigger.

Johnston stared at the man. "I don't even know you. What makes you think I would trust you?"

"Does it have to be you watching?" I interrupted. "Can't somebody else from the company be with Mario while he works?"

"It would have to be someone who has a high enough security clearance to see the information on the computer."

"Who would that be?"

"My senior executives. The people at yesterday's meeting: Samantha Macabee and Donny Sackett."

"As we talked about yesterday, everybody's a suspect in the killing, even those two. They shouldn't even know about Mario or this computer." I would have started pacing the room at that moment; I like to pace while I think. Unfortunately, pacing this room would have put me out in the hall. Suddenly it hit me. "They weren't the only ones at the meeting."

Mikah looked at me for a few seconds, then a smile slowly came to his face.

Thirty minutes later, Mario was seated at another desk, Goodwin's computer facing him. Seated at her own desk next to him was Jenny.

Neither person looked happy.

Chapter 9

As we were getting Mario situated in Jenny's office, I took the opportunity to fill Johnston in on all the latest news of my investigation. That included the gossip I had picked up the night before from Sammy Brackens regarding Goodwin, women and cars, not to mention the evening's shooting and this morning's discovery of the missing computer. Mikah made sure I wasn't hiding any bullet wounds from him, then addressed the results of my night's work.

"Two bad bits of news and one possibly good bit," commented Johnston. "The good part being Goodwin possibly having a girlfriend. Are you going to try finding her?"

"Definitely," I answered. "But you're wrong about there being two bad news items. The loss of the computer by the police actually may be good for us."

"How's that?"

"The message on the computer from Goodwin's home was the same as yesterday's message on our computer. It stands to reason that Goodwin was running the same program on both machines. With their computer missing, the police are now one step behind us. They never got to see the second message; as a matter of fact, they don't even know there is a second message. Besides, they now have to spend time and manpower trying to solve their own case of burglary. That means we have a little more freedom to investigate and a little more time in which to do it."

"Good point," nodded Mikah. "I didn't think of it like that. Although I should remind you, this is not a case of them versus us. It's a case of us helping them. If you discover anything that you can't handle on your own, or results in you getting shot at again, I want you to go the police and have Sarcovich handle it."

"You sure about that, Mikah?" I asked, a note of caution in my voice. "Even if it's something you would rather not be made public knowledge."

"We're talking about murder, Barry. I'm telling you to do what you have to do to catch the murderer, but stay alive in the process. If that means telling the police all you know, tell them." He turned to walk back into his office, but stopped short and turned back toward me. "Just make sure you tell me first."

As Mikah Johnston walked into his office, I turned and walked toward the door leading from the reception area where Jenny's desk was located to the hall. I was headed for the security room and a visit with Charlie McCarthy. As I passed Jenny's desk she didn't look up from her work on her on computer. She was, however, slowly shaking her head and the look on her face told me this evening would probably not be a repeat of last night.

Security was in the basement. For some reason, security is always in the basement. I entered the elevator outside the reception room, found the lowest button on the control panel and pushed it. Sure enough, a few seconds later I was standing outside a door labeled "Cyber Inc. Security Services" and I entered.

The room was much smaller than I had anticipated. I knew that security was responsible not only for the main building, but the three smaller buildings in the industrial park Cyber leased out. As soon as I entered the security offices, I was met by two walls completely covered with television monitors, a quick count showing a total of seventeen. There were four people in Cyber Security uniforms spaced out among the monitors, three men and one woman. I could see from the monitors that some were displaying scenes of the outside of this plant, while others were showing pictures of interiors. The four security personnel were punching keys on wireless keyboards, each punch of a key changing the scene on one of the screens. I recognized a new scene as being the warehouse building. Obviously the monitors were watching all of Cyber Inc.

"How did you get in here?" came a voice off to my right.

I turned and saw man standing in the doorway of another room, from the looks of it another office. The man was about 45 or 50, dark hair and somewhat muscular, although it was obvious that at a younger age he had been much more muscular. He had let himself lose a little of the muscle and replaced it with some fat. I smiled, even though I could tell charm was not going to help me here.

"My name is Barry Dunleavy. I'm a private investigator hired by Cyber to investigate the murder of Larry Goodwin."

The man looked me over for a few seconds, his eyes not exactly showing a strong enthusiasm at seeing me. "I didn't ask who you are, I asked how you got here. I figured you would be Dunleavy."

"I took the elevator."

"Are you some kind of wise ass? Everybody takes the elevator; there's no other way to get down here. I want to know who gave you clearance to come in here."

"I have clearance to go anywhere in the plant," I answered, a slight edge in my voice. It wasn't even noon yet, and I had already had a long day. I didn't feel like putting up with an arrogant flunky.

"Nobody comes into this office without some kind of warning phone call or signal, not even me." He emphasized the "me," as if the "me" was somebody special. "Whoever told you to come down here was supposed to let us know. What's the jerk's name so I can give him a lesson in protocol."

"His name is Johnston. Mikah Johnston."

The man looked at me for a second, then turned back into his office. "Get in here, Dunleavy," he called back.

I followed, smiling to myself that I had managed to shut this guy up. As I entered the office, the man was just sitting down in an old swivel chair behind a large metallic green desk. There was a nameplate sitting on the desk that read "C. H. McCarthy, Director of Security." The man motioned for me to shut the door behind me, which I did.

"If people would just follow the rules they approved, I could do my job. We wouldn't have people getting murdered around here and we wouldn't need people like you nosing around."

I figured if McCarthy was going to be a schmuck I might as well play the game. Courtesy went out the window. No explanations, no requests.

"I need to see your sign-in logs for yesterday and the day before," I said, not bothering to sit in the chair McCarthy didn't offer me.

"Oh, you do, do you?" he said as he leaned back in the old metal swivel chair. "Just who the hell do you think you are, demanding anything of me?"

I walked over to the desk and stood across from the security man. I bent down and put my hands on the desk.

"Who am I? I'm the guy who has been told by the CEO of this company to go wherever I have to, do whatever I have to in order find the person who killed Larry Goodwin. You are the man, just like every other employee of this company, who has been told to cooperate with me and do whatever I ask. Now do your job and get those logs." I then turned, grabbed the chair in front of McCarthy's desk and sat down.

McCarthy leaned forward in his chair and stood up, all in one motion. His face was beet red, either from anger or from embarrassment at being talked to like that, I wasn't sure which and I really didn't care. My voice had been loud enough to carry through the thin glass window of McCarthy's office so the four security guards watching the monitors had heard every word I said. McCarthy wasn't moving; he just stood there, his face getting redder every second and his beefy hands opening and closing into massive fists. He dearly wanted to hit me, but you could see he was thinking over the three things that could result from him taking a swing at me. He could beat me to a pulp and throw me out his office; he could beat me to a pulp, throw me out of his office and then be fired for not cooperating with me like he had been ordered; or he could take a swing at me, I would beat him to a pulp, take the log books and then have him fired for not cooperating with me like he had been ordered. Three choices, two bad outcomes and only one good. Had it been ten years earlier he might have chosen to fight; but now he had a good job and was ten years closer to retirement. He made a fourth choice.

"Wait here and I'll get the logs," he mumbled, and I noticed a bit of sag to his shoulders.

I watched the security chief walk out of his office and go up to a row of filing cabinets on the wall across from the monitors. I could also see the heads of the four security guards swivel as their eyes followed him. His back was to them and I could see they were all smiling. Obviously, I hadn't been the first person McCarthy had attempted to bully, but I might have been the first to bully him back. As he turned away from the filing drawer with a book in his hand, he eyed his guards. They had quickly turned back to the monitors and made as if they were actually watching what was happening. McCarthy walked back into his office, threw the book on the desk in front of me and sat back down in his chair.

"But that book," he said pointing to the ledger he had retrieved from the filing cabinet, "doesn't leave this office. Those are my orders and I follow orders."

"Fine with me," I answered, not bothering to look up from the book I had just opened. I was flipping through the pages, looking for two things: the time Goodwin signed out two nights earlier and the time he signed in yesterday. I turned to the page marked Monday, April 18, two days ago. After scanning the page, I found Goodwin's entry: he had signed out at 11:55 p.m. I flipped to the page for yesterday. There was no entry for Goodwin. I double checked, but still found no entry. Well, that explained one thing. I closed the book and flipped it back onto the desk in front of McCarthy.

"I need a photocopy of the entries for the last two days."

McCarthy grabbed the book from the desk, crossed the room to where he had a small desktop copier and ran off the copies I had requested. He brought them back to me and threw them on his desk. "Anything else?" he asked.

"No," I answered as I rose from my chair and turned to leave.

"Dunleavy!" said the security chief.

I turned back and watched the man walk from behind his desk. He stopped with his face less than a foot from mine, and he was smiling.

"One of these days you and I will meet on the street. Then I won't be an employee of Cyber and you won't be Johnston's little helper. That's when we'll have a little 'discussion' about what went on in here today."

"Fine," I said. I turned, walked out of his office and up to the door leading into the hallway. That's when I stopped and turned back to McCarthy. "Just make sure when we have our discussion you move your lips so I know it's you talking."

As I walked out of the room I thought I heard one of the guards snicker.

After checking on Mario and finding out that he was, in his opinion, hours away from getting into Goodwin's program, I decided to leave; I'd come back for him later. I wanted to check with Fred and see how his missing computer case was coming. Not that the fact it was missing interested me. It had occurred to me, however, that the name Phil Morrissey had come up twice in the last twenty-four hours, both times in connection with Larry Goodwin. Morrissey was the cop in charge of the Property room when the computer was lifted, and he was also the cop mentioned by Sammy Bracken as the one who saw Goodwin driving the red sports car with the beautiful black-haired woman. My, what a coincidence!

I had been doing my thinking as I was walking from Jenny's office to the front entrance of the Cyber administrative offices. I walked out into the bright noonday sun of yet another beautiful Berkshire spring day. I smelled the lilac bushes on either side of the entranceway and felt a small pang at the thought that they would be dead when a normal frost hit, probably some time within the next week. But as I said, I'm not much into foliage, so I returned to my thoughts.

Goodwin had signed out of the plant Monday night. He never signed back in after that, but yet he was found dead in the administrative building of the plant on Tuesday morning. That led to several questions. Where had he gone after he signed out on Monday? Not home. I knew that because both the sink and bathtub of his apartment were dry. Even if he hadn't showered Tuesday morning, he would have at least run the water in his sink to brush his teeth, comb his hair or whatever. Had he stayed with the woman he was seen with while driving the red sports car? Come to think of it, where was that car? Come to think of it, who was the woman? And finally, how did he get back into the plant without signing the logbook?

Two of my questions, the ones about the car and the woman, were answered just then. As I stood on the steps to the plant entrance, I saw a red sports car drive up to the security shack, stop a moment, then get waved through. The driver navigated into one of the reserved parking spaces next to the building, shut off the car and got out. She was a beautiful woman with black hair, the same kind of woman Phil Morrissey told Sammy Brackens he saw with Larry Goodwin riding in a red sports car several weeks earlier. The woman walked over to the steps and stopped in front of me.

"Hello, Mr. Dunleavy," she said, her voice just as sharp but sultry as I remembered. "Making any progress in your investigation?

"Why, yes I am, Ms. Macabee," I answered. "And it's funny you should ask. Can we go to your office and talk?"

"I really have no idea what you're talking about, Mr. Dunleavy," said Samantha Macabee as she sat in the plush chair behind her office desk five minutes later. I was standing just inside the door, having stopped to take in the view of what passed for a senior executive's office. Macabee's chair sat behind a large mahogany desk, which sat in front of a picture window looking out on the manicured lawns of the plant's backside. The room itself, paneled and just slightly smaller than Mikah Johnston's, smelled of the financial officer's perfume. Just before we had reached her office I had broached the subject of she and Goodwin driving around town together.

"You were seen in your little red car, with Goodwin driving."

"If that's true, why wouldn't I be driving my own car?"

"You were too busy running your fingers through Goodwin's hair. Good driving protocol requires you have at least one hand on the steering wheel at all times."

Macabee leaned back in her chair, the smile on her face dropping a little for half a second, but it was back quickly enough. "I was seen, you say? Obviously not by you. Do you always listen to gossip as a means of investigating your cases?"

"Yes," I answered crossing the room and seating myself in the chair in front of her desk. "Especially when the one spreading the gossip is a Pittsfield city cop." I didn't bother telling her my gossip came second hand from another cop.

"I don't know any policemen personally, Mr. Dunleavy. How could one recognize me?"

"He didn't," I explained. "He recognized Goodwin, who was a fairly prominent college athlete before he came to work for Cyber. The cop knew what he looked like and knew that he worked in Pittsfield."

"So where do I come into this picture?"

"Goodwin didn't own a red sports car, so it probably belonged to the black-haired woman riding with him. Now what woman did Goodwin know who has black hair and drives a red sports car?"

Macabee stared at me for what seemed like an hour, but was probably no more than 15 seconds at most. Then she let out an almost inaudible sigh.

"Very well, Mr. Dunleavy. You're right. It was me."

"So you and Goodwin were a little more than employee-supervisor, I take it."

"A delicate way to put it, thank you. Larry and I were having an affair."

"Why didn't you bring that up at yesterday's meeting?"

She let out a rough laugh. "You are kidding, aren't you? Tell Mikah Johnston I was sleeping with an employee thirteen years my junior? I don't think that would have gone over very well. I don't know how well you know Mikah, but he's a bit old fashioned. Besides, he wouldn't like the image it gave the company."

"This is a murder investigation, you know," I answered. "It would have been nice if you were truthful."

"You're not a cop anymore, Mr. Dunleavy. I don't have to be honest with you." She stood up and walked over to the window. "If and when the police ask me about my relationship with Larry Goodwin I will tell them everything. I'm hoping it won't come to that. I'm hoping you'll find the killer before it comes to that."

"In order to protect you career. Sounds like you and Goodwin had a wonderful relationship."

She turned around quickly and shot me the same look she had given me the day before in the conference room when I had first laid eyes on her.

"Our relationship was strictly physical. He enjoyed being with me and sharing my… lifestyle; I enjoyed being around someone younger than myself and flattered that I was still attractive enough to entice someone like Larry. He was young, good-looking and virile."

"He was your 'boy toy.'"

She smiled. "If that's the way you prefer to think of it, then yes. There was no love involved, and so there was no way I was going to jeopardize my career by volunteering information."

I shook my head and slowly stood up. "Lady, I don't care if you sleep with half of Berkshire County if it makes you feel good. But now that I know about you and Goodwin, I want your complete cooperation in this investigation."

"Are you going to tell Johnston?" For the first time her voice held a touch of emotion—fear.

"Only if it relates to the murder. If not, what he doesn't know won't hurt him."

She visibly relaxed. "How can I help you?"

"You can start by answering some questions. How long had you and Goodwin been having this affair?"

"About a month, maybe five weeks."

Did you know about Goodwin's gambling problem?"

She looked shocked. "He had a gambling problem?"

"He owed over one hundred grand to a not-so-nice bookie."

She shook her head slowly. "My God," she mumbled, "that's probably why he never had much money. He almost never picked up a check when we went out."

That's also probably why he picked a successful woman like Macabee to fool around with, regardless of her looks; hopefully, for her sake, it would be awhile before she hit on that idea as well.

"Speaking of which," I said, "where did you two go when you went out?"

"Obviously not in Pittsfield," she smiled. "It wouldn't be a good idea to be accidentally seen by someone I knew. We usually headed for out-of-town places. We would go to small restaurants or bars in Great Barrington or Williamstown, sometimes even Springfield or Albany."

"Are you sure no one you knew ever saw you together?"

"I was very careful."

"Anyone Goodwin know ever see you together?"

Macabee frowned, her mind obviously thinking back. "Not that I can remem...wait a minute! I don't know if this means anything, but it was about two weeks ago at Damancey's."

"I don't think I know it," I said.

"That's because it's in Albany. It's kind of a flashy, up-scale bar. Larry and I walked in and the bartender looked at Larry and smiled. Then he looked at me and frowned slightly. Then he shrugged his shoulders and went about his business. I thought it was somewhat strange, but I just let it go. I don't know if it means anything."

"I don't either, but it might. Do you have any photos of you and Goodwin?"

She smiled and shook her head slightly. "I would never let our picture be taken together. I'm sure you can understand my reasons."

"Yes, I do. One last question for now: were you with Goodwin Monday night, the night before he died?"

She shook her head. "No, we were originally supposed to meet at my place at seven and then go to Springfield for dinner. Around four that afternoon he called my office and said something had come up and he had to work late. We rescheduled for Tuesday night."

"Okay, Ms. Macabee," I said, standing up, "if I need anything else I'll be in touch."

I turned to leave, but I stopped suddenly. I looked on the wall that had been to my right as I was seated. On the wall, surrounding Macabee's several diplomas, was a series of framed photographs. Most were group shots, but not the kind you see on most people's walls. Those have smiling, casually dressed people mugging for the camera and smiling to beat the band. The pictures on this wall were of people in business attire, and the expressions on their faces said, "Okay, I'll give you a courtesy smile, but I really think this is stupid." Most of the photos showed Macabee in a group with either Johnston or Donny Sackett or both, along with other people who were obviously clients. One of the pictures caught my eye.

"When was this picture taken?" I asked as I crossed to the wall and pointed.

Macabee came over next to me. "About six or seven months ago. We had just completed contract negotiations with the city and were at the contract signing. As you can see from the photo, there's Mayor Thomasson, Assistant Mayor Randall, Parks Department Supervisor Peterson..."

"Why was he there?"

"Who, Mr. Peterson? The contract called for Cyber to create a software package to oversee the Parks and Recreation Department budget and staffing needs. But tell me, what's so special about this picture?"

"Standing in the back is Larry Goodwin."

Macabee looked back at the photograph. "So he is. As a matter of fact, I remember now that he was present at the contract signing."

"Why?" I asked. "Isn't it unusual for a junior programmer,

101

especially one who at that time had been with Cyber Inc. for two months, to be at a contract signing with the bigwigs of the company and the city government?"

"Larry was a star college athlete and, after all, this was a deal with the city recreation department. It was a natural tie-in and it made for a good public relations moment. That's the only reason he was included."

I reached up and took the photograph off the wall.

"What are you doing?" asked the woman.

"I need a picture with both you and Goodwin in it together. This is it." I took the photograph out of the frame, which I handed to Macabee. "Besides," I added, "you should be happy. You're both in the photograph, but you're not together; kind of like your relationship with Goodwin."

I assume Macabee gave me her best Ice Princess stare, but I don't really know. As I was making my statement, I turned and walked out of the room.

Chapter 10

It was past noon and since Mario still hadn't figured out the Goodwin computer program I decided to head out for a bite of lunch. I made my way to Fenn Street and the Berkshire Café. Everything around this county has the word 'Berkshire' in its name, like the Berkshire Museum and the Berkshire Athenaeum (which, I discovered a few years ago, is just a fancy word for "library"). If there had been a bordello in town it probably would have been called the "Berkshire Bawdy House and Chicken Ranch." I don't know who settled this area, but it had to be people with absolutely no imagination, and over the last two hundred years any imagination they did have had been bred out of their descendants. Anyway, the Berkshire Café serves good burgers, great coffee and fresh newspapers; it was the newspaper I wanted more than the other two items.

Fifteen minutes after leaving the Cyber parking lot, I was settled into a booth, had placed my order and was reading the front page of the *Berkshire Guardian* (see, I told you!). I figured the murder would be front-page news and I was right. I was more interested than anything else in seeing how they would play up the angle that it was a Cyber employee that was murdered and not the typical west end drug dealer. Like I had anticipated, the *Guardian* played it to the hilt. "Cyber Exec Executed!" rang the headline. If Goodwin was an executive then I was the police chief; but then the *Guardian* never let facts get in the way of a good story or headline. I skimmed the initial paragraphs since I knew most of the facts of the case and concentrated on the parts of the article that centered on the police investigation. Other than the big play given Goodwin's gambling habit (which I had expected), there wasn't a whole lot going on according to the article, at least that was what Sarcovich was saying. The police were questioning people who knew Goodwin (hopefully more people than just Tre Barker, the dead man's former landlord), but had as yet not found anyone who had been with the deceased the night before his murder.

The most interesting part of the newspaper article I managed to find was on page four, where the article continued. Next to a sidebar with the headline "Larry Goodwin, All-American, Found Dead" (a bio piece about Goodwin's days as a Berkshire County star athlete), the main piece talked about the autopsy results. Sarcovich had the autopsy crammed in ahead of others on the waiting list because this was such a high profile case. According to the coroner, Goodwin was killed between midnight and 6 a.m., although she felt it might be closer to the midnight end. I concurred, not because I'm any type of medical wiz who can look at a corpse and tell you the exact time of death, but because I can read a logbook. What also made the autopsy article interesting was what was not in it. Goodwin had been shot, but with what type of gun? That was a no-brainer piece of information in any autopsy report, but the paper made no mention of it. I made a mental note to ask Fred Martin at our next meeting.

My burger came while I scanning the paper for any more news on the investigation. I didn't find any, so I put it down, picked up the burger and was just about to bite into it when I heard, "Hey, Barry! Fancy meeting you here!"

I turned around to see Donny Sackett making his way to my table. I said hello when he reached me but didn't bother to ask him to sit. He sat anyway and I resigned myself to having company at lunch.

"How are you making out with the investigation?" he asked, eyeing my burger in a way that made me take a big bite out of it quickly; the thought that it might not be around much longer had suddenly made me hungry.

"Pretty good," I answered in a non-committal tone. "Slow, but steady."

"Good," he said as he reached over to my plate and grabbed a pickle. "Do you mind? I'm starved!"

"So order yourself something."

"Good idea," he said, oblivious to the sarcasm in the suggestion. He waved the waitress over, gave her an order that duplicated mine, only he changed the coffee to beer, and watched her walk away. "Nice ass," he muttered as she sashayed to the kitchen.

I didn't look up from my burger or bother to answer, but the conversation didn't lapse; Sackett saw to that.

"So you think you're getting closer?"

"To what?"

"To finding the killer?"

"Nope," I mumbled, a large portion of the burger having found its way into my mouth.

"But you just said the investigation was going well," he said in a confused voice. "How can it be going well if your not zeroing in on the killer?"

I took a sip of coffee, slowly took the napkin off my lap and wiped my mouth with it, then replaced the napkin. It was only then that I looked at Sackett.

"Solving a crime has two parts to it," I began in my most professorial tone of voice. "The first part involves the investigation. That's where you gather clues, as many as you can, as fast as you can and in no particular order. The second part involves deduction. You sort the clues you worked so hard to gather into some sort of picture, build time frames of people and events and begin to construct scenarios. I'm currently in the investigation process. I've found things out and discovered some clues that may or may not be important. That part is going well. I haven't even bothered with the deduction part yet."

Sackett stared at me with a blank look on his face, either out of confusion or disappointment I wasn't sure which. And I didn't care which. He was a suspect in the murder and I wasn't going to give him the least bit of information.

"Oh, sure," he stammered after a few seconds. "That makes sense. Never really thought of it like that."

"So you want to help me with the investigation part?" I asked suddenly.

"Uh, sure!" he said, taken by surprise by the question. "What can I do?"

"Tell me where you were Monday night?"

"Monday? But Larry was killed Tuesday morning!"

"Then you won't mind telling me about Monday."

"Okay," he shrugged. "I don't mind at all. Monday night I worked until about eleven or so, went home and went to bed."

"What did you work on?" I asked.

"Just putting some finishing touches on a contract with the state."

"You work that late often?"

"Quite often. That's why I'm the best in the business." He smiled.

"Goodwin worked late that night too," I said. "Did you see him?"

The smile left his face. "Yeah," Sackett answered. "He was working on another one of our projects and he came into my office once or twice to get approvals on what he was doing."

"Which was it: once or twice?"

"What does that matter?"

"It may not matter at all. I'm just gathering information."

Sackett thought for a second. "Twice. No! Three times actually. Once around seven-thirty, once again around eight and a final time at eleven."

"How do you remember the times?"

"The first time he came in just as I was returning from the break room with a microwaved dinner and I remember seeing the time on the microwave oven. The second time because he came in asking the same questions he asked a half-hour earlier and that bothered me. The third time was right after I looked at my watch and decided it was time to call it a night."

"What did Goodwin want the third time?" I asked.

"He came in to tell me he thought he was finished with the project he was working on and that he had started a new one. He wanted me to look at it. I told him I was leaving and would see it in the morning." Sackett stopped, gave a thoughtful look and then added, "Funny."

"What's funny?"

"Larry seemed, well, upset that I wouldn't go look at what he was doing. But all he did was mumble something like "Okay, see you in the morning," then walked back to his office. I didn't think much about it. I just went home."

"Well." I smiled as I got up and took the last long gulp of my coffee. "It should give you something to chew over besides that burger you ordered. Have a nice lunch." And with that I stood up, dropped enough money on the table to pay the bill and leave the waitress a nice tip, turned and walked out of the café.

It was 1 p.m. I knew what I wanted to do and where to go, only that wasn't going to be possible until later in the evening, so I settled on a trip to the local electronics store at the mall. I felt that if the Goodwin's personal computer from home was valuable enough to steal, people might just want to get their hands on his company computer at Cyber as well. I needed something to grab a possible thief's attention and keep him from snatching the computer before Mario had cracked the code. I found it at The Electronics Store (not a very imaginative name, but at least it didn't have the word "Berkshire" in it). By 2:15 p.m. I had my secret weapon in the trunk of my car (along with a receipt that I definitely would be turning in with my expense account) and was headed back to downtown Pittsfield.

By the time I hit Waconah Street, just ten minutes from the Cyber plant, I had Jenny on my cell phone.

"How's Mario coming along?" I asked when she picked up the line.

"Fine," she answered in a light voice. "He's actually not as bad as I originally thought; still not the kind of guy I would want to work with everyday, but that's not going to happen anyway."

"That's nice," I answered somewhat sarcastically, "but I was asking how he was coming along with the computer, not with you."

"If you'll hang on a second, I'll put him on the line and you can ask him yourself."

A moment later, Mario's voice came onto the phone. "That you, Barry?"

"Yeah, and since when is it 'Barry' instead of 'Dunleavy'? When did we get on a first name basis?"

"Hey, if you can't be friends with a guy who sends you to jail, introduces you to a beautiful woman and puts three hundred bucks in your pocket, who can you be friends with?"

"I'm not your friend, I'm your boss and this is strictly business. Now if you want to make that three hundred then keep working. I have some people to see. I'll pick you up at four if I don't hear from you before then. If you need me, Ms. St. Pierre has my cell number."

I hung up on him. I really liked Mario and could see myself being friends with him, except Mario had a little personality flaw: he liked to use people. The best way to handle Mario was to use him.

I turned onto First Street and then over to Fenn and parked in a lot across from City Hall. That wasn't where I wanted to go, however. My destination was a small, paved alleyway next to the police station between Allen and North Streets. The city had taken to putting flowers and benches on the asphalt, I assume in order to designate it a city park. I took a seat on one of the benches, pulled out my cell phone and dialed the number. After only one ring there came a familiar voice.

"Detective Martin speaking. How may I help you?"

"You can get your butt out from behind your desk, walk out the front door of the station and meet me in the alleyway next door."

"I'm supposed to drop whatever I'm doing and just come out to have a little chat? I don't know about you, Barry, but I'm a little busy."

"Too busy for an exchange of information about Goodwin?" There was silence on the other end. "How big of an exchange?" "Big enough to stop us spinning our wheels and get us both moving in positive directions," I answered. "So are you game?"

In less than four minutes Fred was seated next to me on the bench. "What have you got?" he asked.

"Not so fast," I smiled. "We need to agree on the ground rules first. I'll give you a little something, then you give me a little something. We'll keep volleying until one of us gets tired and walks away. Sound good?"

"Alright," agreed Fred, nodding his head. "Tit for tat. You go first."

"Okay, try this one on for size: Larry Goodwin signed out of Cyber just before midnight on the night before he died, but he never signed back in. How did he end up dead on the break room floor if he never re-entered the plant?"

"You sure about this?" asked Fred.

"Positive," I answered.

"That's interesting. We've been concentrating on his movements away from the plant, so we hadn't gotten to the log books yet at Cyber."

"So I just saved you a lot of time. Now it's your turn. What's happening with the lost computer?"

"Still lost. We got hold of Morrissey at his apartment around eight-thirty. He says he left that cage only once on his entire shift. He went to the bathroom around two o'clock this morning. He knows he's supposed to lock the place up when he leaves and he says he did. We've checked with everyone else who worked the late shift and no one remembers anybody going near the cage. You have anything else?"

"Well," I said, "besides being a gambler, Goodwin was a ladies man."

Fred's eyebrows shot up. "Any lady in particular?"

"I haven't found one, yet," I lied. "But this whole affair is starting to look very interesting. Here we have a dead man who worked on government contracts, but he was also a gambler and a womanizer.

Goodwin is beginning to sound like a man on the make, and that opens the door to a lot of possibilities."

"It would make life easier if there weren't so many doors," sighed Fred, leaning back on the bench.

"Well, it's your turn to give," I said. "Why was there no information on the type of gun used in the murder in the newspaper report? You and I know that kind of information usually gets big play."

Fred looked at me, and then craned his neck from side to side to make sure nobody was in listening distance. "This definitely stays under your hat, Barry."

"I promise," I said, wondering what could be so important that Fred was getting paranoid over telling me.

"The bullet came from the same gun that was used in another murder."

I gave a low whistle. "So you're keeping that information from the public."

"That's right," nodded Fred. "Finding that gun and matching it to Goodwin's killer may solve another open murder case on the books."

"So who's the other murder victim?"

"Remember that hotshot entrepreneur up in North County that was found dead in his house last year? Roger Phelps?"

"Yeah, I remember the story. He just got this dot-com startup going, was beginning to do well with it, and then boom: he shows up dead."

"I'm afraid so. What are the odds?"

I sat there a moment, disgusting the new information. Then I said, "Speaking of odds, I didn't get any good vibes when I talked to Vinnie Lombardi. I don't think he had anything to do with Goodwin's murder."

"Funny you should mention Lombardi."

"Why's that?"

"The car that held whoever took those pot shots at you last night might be linked to Lombardi. We canvassed the area, talking to the residents. Some old guy was taking out his garbage, heard the shots and then saw this car shoot by like a bat out of hell."

"Was it a Honda?" I asked, remembering the car that sped away from Mikal's with the two shooters.

"This guy wouldn't know a Honda from a Ford, he says. But he managed to get a partial on the license plate, the first three numbers."

"And...?"

"Now you don't think Lombardi's going to take a shot at you from a car with his personal plates on it, do you?"

"So what makes you think Lombardi was involved?"

"We checked the reports on stolen cars and it seems that a dark blue Honda with plates that match the first three digits the old man gave us was stolen in North Adams late yesterday afternoon."

"So are you going to go talk to Vinnie?"

"You may not need a reason to hassle Lombardi, Barry," Fred shrugged, "but the police do. We looked into his whereabouts last night, and he has two witnesses that say he was with them."

"His two goons?" I sneered. "They were the ones who took the shots at me."

"And Lombardi swears he was with them all day and night."

"Cozy. But the fact remains, I don't think they were in on Goodwin's death. It cost Lombardi a big payday when the kid died."

I paused a couple of seconds, waiting for the Lombardi issue to die a silent, slow death. It was then that I asked the question I needed answered, the question that was the reason for my little sparring session with Fred.

"What can you tell me about Goodwin's car?"

I knew I would never get near the vehicle as long as the investigation was going on; Sarcovich would see to that. But with the discovery that Goodwin had signed out of Cyber at midnight the night before he died, never signed back in but was found dead at the plant the next morning, his means of transportation during that time was just as important to me as where he was for that missing six hour period.

"What happened to our little tit for tat?" asked Fred with a grin. "I just gave you info on Lombardi."

"That was about my being shot at; it had nothing to do with the Goodwin murder," I rejoined. "Besides, I started that conversation with information on Lombardi not probably being involved with the murder. I believe it's your turn to give me something."

"Fine," shrugged Fred. "It's funny you should ask, because there's something strange about that car."

"Strange how?"

"We brought it down to the impound yard and stripped it to the bone. We found nothing. No blood, no dirt and no fingerprints anywhere, not even on the steering wheel."

"Which means..." I began.

"Which means somebody wiped it clean so we wouldn't find anything if we looked."

"Then the car was used for something we're not supposed to know about."

"That's the way we figure it," said Fred. "But if you're going to transport a dead body in a car, erasing all the evidence isn't that easy. There should have been a drop of blood, a hair follicle, some skin, something. But there wasn't."

"Maybe it wasn't a dead body they were transporting," I offered.

"Then what was it?"

"I have no idea," I said, rising to my feet. "But you'll be the..."

"I know," interrupted Fred. "...the first to know. I've heard that before."

I had gotten as much out of my ex-partner as I was going to get for awhile, so I meandered across Allen Street to City Hall. Marcus would be up on the latest regarding the killing, and I was sure he wouldn't be as hesitant as Fred Martin to fill me in. All I had to do was come up with an excuse for Molly to let me in to see the mayor for ten minutes. I was saved that dilemma. As I was making my way up the steps to the front door to the building, out came Marcus and Melissa Randal, both of their sets of arms packed with folders. Randal must have caught her heel on something, because she stumbled forward but caught herself before falling. However, the folders in her arms went flying, scattering down the steps. I caught as many papers on the fly as I could, then stooped to retrieve the one on the ground. Marcus went flying after some that had been caught by the wind and were lightly wafting down Allen Street.

"Oh, thank you, Mr. Dunleavy. That was so clumsy of me," said Melissa Randal, also chasing after the fallen documents.

I handed her the papers I had collected, and as she reached out to take them I noticed the ring on her right hand. It was a class ring.

"I didn't know you graduated from MCLA?" I said.

"Attended, not graduated. I transferred to UMASS. But how did you know…?"

I pointed to her ring. "That's why I'm a detective." I smiled. "I notice things like that. And by the way, it's 'Barry.'"

"Barry!" Marcus smiled as he spotted me. "How are you?" He handed Melissa Randal all the documents he had grabbed on his run.

"Pretty good, Mr. Mayor," I replied in a light voice. "And how are you, Ms. Randal?"

"I'm just fine, thank you, Barry," answered the assistant mayor.

"It looks like you two are off to another meeting."

"Just across the street," Marcus answered, nodding his head in the direction of the police station. "Budget time coming up and we have to go over the police figures."

"So how come the chief doesn't come to you hat in hand?"

"He's busy with the Cyber investigation, so we volunteered to go to him," said Randal. "Besides, his initial budget request included large maintenance items for the police station itself, so Marcus and I can use the time to look around the building."

"I'd invite you to walk with us and chat, Barry," smiled the mayor, "but it's about a twenty-second walk and besides, you're not the most welcome of visitors to Police Chief Sarcovich's police station."

"That's okay, Marcus. I already had my yearly visit yesterday. But before you go, there is just one question I would like to ask both of you concerning the Goodwin case."

"What's that, Barry?"

"How well did either of you know Goodwin?"

"I never met him," answered the mayor, somewhat taken aback

by the question. "At least I don't think I have. Did you know him, Melissa?"

"No, Marcus," answered the young woman. " I'm pretty sure we didn't run in the same circles."

"The reason I ask," I said as I reached into the breast pocket of my sport coat and pulled out the photo I had taken from Samantha Macabee's office, "is that the two of you are in the same photograph with Goodwin."

"Really?" said Marcus. "Here, let me see."

I handed him the photograph and he and Melissa Randal both stared at it for a moment. Then Marcus looked up and handed the picture back to me.

"I seem to remember now," said the Mayor. "It was at the official signing of a contract between the city recreation department and Cyber. Goodwin was there and I shook his hand, but I never spoke with him. Did you, Melissa?"

"I think I had a polite conversation, but that was about it. If I remember correctly, Goodwin was there more in his capacity as a former football player than anything that had to do with the contract. It was a little public relations moment for Cyber so we didn't object to him being there."

"Well, thanks for your time," I said as I put the photograph back in my pocket. "I don't want to keep you from your important meeting with the chief."

"You're all heart, Barry," smiled Marcus. "Will I see you at Jake's later?"

"Probably not," I said. "I have to get back to Cyber for awhile, then I'm headed out of town to track down a lead."

"Anything you'd like to fill me in on?"

"Not right now, Marcus. Perhaps later."

"Suit yourself." With that he and Melissa Randal crossed Allen Street and entered the police station.

Chapter 11

I was about to commit a crime. I know what you're thinking: I used to be a cop and should know better, and the fact that I was trying to solve a murder case didn't give me the right to break the law. I sat in my car on the way to Cyber Inc. and thought about those things, but only for a block or two, then I quickly put them out of my mind. The hardest part of my plan was that I had to involve Jenny in it, and while she agreed to help I knew it went against everything she believed in. She was loyal to Cyber, and she was especially loyal to Mikah Johnston. She didn't like going against his orders, even to help me.

By the time I reached the front gates of Cyber and was admitted to the plant, Jenny and Mario DeRigger, whose help I also needed, were waiting, having already performed their part. I had called them on my cell phone as Marcus and Melissa Randal were walking into the police station and informed them of my plan. They had packed up the computer Mario had spent the day working on in a nondescript brown box and had brought it to the back loading dock via the service elevator. I drove directly there, parked next to the platform occupied by Jenny, Mario and the computer and parked the car. Jumping out, I ran to the back of my car and opened the trunk. I grabbed the computer from Mario and placed it in the trunk, covering it with a blanket. Then I removed another box, which held an exact duplicate of the computer I was stealing. My trip to the electronics store at the mall, while an expensive outing, was going to keep anyone from stealing Goodwin's Cyber computer like they stole his laptop from the police. Besides, I could always put the cost of the computer on my expense account.

I handed Mario the duplicate computer and, while he and Jenny returned to the executive suite via the same service elevator, I returned my car to the front of the plant and parked in my usual visitor's spot. I then entered the building and took the regular elevator up to the top floor. Stepping out, I saw Mario just finish attaching the new computer to the monitor. As far as anyone else knew, this was the same computer he had been working at all day.

I collected Mario, said goodbye to Jenny and was about to take my leave when the elevator doors opened and Mikah Johnston and Donny Sackett walked into the executive suite foyer.

"Hello, Barry," Johnston said, his usual smile looking a little more forced than usual. "How's the investigation coming?"

"Actually, Mikah," I answered, grabbing Mario's arm and steering him toward the elevator, "it's going quite well. I'm almost ready to begin Phase Two." I looked at Sackett and smiled.

"Well, I guess that's a good thing," said a confused Johnston. "How did Mr. DeRigger make out with Goodwin's computer?" Sackett's head shot up when he heard the question.

"Goodwin's computer? What about his computer, Mikah?"

"Barry's friend here has been looking into the computer files in an attempt to find something for us."

"Mikah," stammered Sackett, visibly upset, "Goodwin's computer holds quite a few classified files and documents. I don't think…"

"Don't worry, Donny," sighed Johnston. "That computer has never left this building and there has been a Cyber employee next to Mr. DeRigger the entire time he has been working on it."

Sackett turned and looked at Mario, then a moment later at me. I smiled and waved as the elevator doors shut.

"You know, Dunleavy," said Mario as we were seated in my car traveling down East Street, "I don't think three hundred bucks is going to cover the cost of the lawyer I'm going to need when they throw me in jail for stealing a computer. This was grand theft, a felony. Believe me, I know a felony when I commit one."

"Relax, Mario, no one is going to jail. After you figure out a way to get Goodwin's computer to give the name of his killer, Mikah Johnston will be so happy he may give you the damn thing. Just as soon as he wipes out all the classified files, that is."

"So now what?"

"I take you home," I explained. "For a few hours, that is, while I take this computer to my place. I have to go out of town, but I should be back around nine o'clock tonight. You be ready by then and I'll pick you up, bring you to the computer and let you work on it all night if you have to. I suggest you get some sleep; you may need it. And if you're lucky, when I bring you to my place I may even feed you."

"Great, just don't make it Chinese. I hate Chinese!"

I dropped off Mario at his place, pulled a U-turn and headed back west to my house. For what I had to do tonight, I figured a shower and shave were in order. Twenty minutes later I had pulled into my garage, grabbed the computer from the trunk and was headed up my walk when my neighbor, Mrs. Prevety, yelled out from her front window.

"Hey, Barry! You had a visitor today!"

"Did he leave a name?" I called back.

"Didn't need to, it was the police. He came right after you left with your friend this morning. Said he was checking up on last night's incident. What happened last night, Barry?"

Mrs. Prevety was a nice old lady who looked out for my house while I was off working. Unfortunately, she looked after my house when I was at home, as well—nosy, but nice. If I told her about being shot at the night before she would be all over me for the details, and right now I didn't have the time.

"Nothing much, Mrs. Prevety. I just witnessed a crime, gave a report to the police. They probably just wanted to check on a few of the details."

"They must have more than a few details to cover," she said. "When you didn't answer the front door, the cop went around back. Then he came around front again and down the far side of your house. He didn't leave until a good fifteen minutes after he got here."

"Is that so?" I mumbled. I was a little concerned now. If the cops wanted me badly enough, they would have been able to contact me through Cyber or Fred Martin. There was no reason to be hanging around my house for fifteen minutes.

I thanked Mrs. Prevety for the news and headed inside the house, but I didn't stay inside long. After hauling Goodwin's computer into my den where I kept my personal computer, I went through my living room, into the kitchen and out the rear door leading to my small back yard. I looked around, but didn't notice anything missing or out of the ordinary. Then I made my way to the far side of the building, away from Mrs. Prevety's place. It was the side all of my electrical and phones lines came into the house. I spent a few minutes looking around, but I couldn't see anything strange. I was about to give up and go back inside for my shower when I noticed a mud pile under the phone junction box. The puddle hadn't dried up in the abnormal spring weather because it was on the side of the house that never got the sun until late afternoon. The puddle was all dug up, as if someone had been sloshing around in it.

The phone box was one that held all the connections leading into the house so the phone people didn't have to go inside. I went over to it and opened the cover. I wasn't sure what I was looking for, not being a phone expert. I didn't need to be one. Being a private investigator, I know something about listening devices, and there was a beauty clamped on one of the lines leading into the house. My phone was bugged!

I retraced my steps and entered the house through the rear door. I went into the bathroom, turned on the shower, got undressed and hopped in. There was no hurry about the phone bug; I wasn't planning on making any secret or urgent calls. But I needed time to think the situation over, and I have found the best place to think is in a hot shower.

Why would the police want to listen in on my conversations? They wouldn't. After all, they don't like it when I talk to them in person, so they wouldn't go out of their way to record me. But there is a big difference between "the police" and a "policeman." There just happened to be one "policeman's" name that kept coming up throughout this investigation; one "policeman" who was unaccounted for this morning around the time the bug had been placed on my line—Phil Morrissey.

But then again, anyone can get a cop's uniform from any costume shop, so why did it have to be a real policeman? Vinnie Lombardi's name was coming up pretty regularly throughout the investigation as well as Morrissey's. The problem was, he was a better bet to shoot me than tap my phone. Maybe he had tried both.

Thinking in a hot shower is great, like I said before, but sooner or later you run out of hot water, which is what happened. So I shut off the jets, dried myself, made some instant coffee and headed into the bedroom to get dressed. I needed to look "up-scale" so I put on some of my best clothes, finished my coffee and headed back out. My destination? Albany's Damancey's bar, where Samantha Macabee and Larry Goodwin had gone a few weeks earlier.

Even though I live in Pittsfield I am only a few miles from the New York State border. I got into my car, pulled back out of driveway, headed down my street about two hundred feet, turned onto Route 20 and headed west. Six minutes later I was in New York and on the way to Albany. I passed through the quaint towns of New Lebanon and Nassau as quickly as the speed limit would allow since I'm not into "quaint" anymore than I'm into apples or foliage. Forty-five minutes after I left my house I was in downtown Albany. Let me rephrase that: I wouldn't be caught dead in downtown Albany unless I wanted to be caught, well, dead! I was actually on Central Avenue as far west of downtown as you can get and still technically in the city.

I found Demancey's easily enough. It was a big, modern gaudy building exuding all the charm neon could exude. It was on the strip between Albany and Schenectady, a strip that used to hold nothing but open fields and now held every franchise store and restaurant you could possibly imagine. I pulled into the parking lot of the "night club" (bar to you and me) and went inside.

If the exterior was gaudy, the interior was more so. The fixtures and bar came right out of some "Bars and Babes" catalog. It was all as modern as you could get; Jake's it was not! But I sucked it up and headed for the bar. A pretty female bartender in white shirt, red bow tie and black vest approached and asked for my order. I felt like I should order some exotic and nasty tasting drink, but I settled on a beer. When she brought it to me I took a sip and then, since I wanted out of there as quickly as possible, came right to the point. I pulled out the picture I had taken from Samantha Macabee's office and, pointing to Larry Goodwin, asked if she recognized him.

"Sorry," she said after spending a long time examining the picture. "Can't say I recognize anybody in this photo. But I've only been here two weeks. You want Ernie over there." She pointed around to the opposite side of the circular bar. "He's been here since the place opened. I'll get him for you." With that she walked over to the man, also dressed in white shirt, red bow tie and black vest, whispered something to him and started chatting with the customer he had been serving. Ernie came over.

"Can I help you, sir?" he asked.

"Yes, I was wondering if you recognize anybody in this picture?" I answered, handing him the photo. He didn't need to spend as much time studying it as his fellow bartender.

"Sure, there's Larry. Don't know his last name, but he's a regular. Comes in all the time."

"Not anymore, he's dead."

"You don't say?" replied the bartender with a little less feeling than a "regular" deserved. "That's too bad. He was a nice guy. We would talk sports a lot, that is when this other chick in the picture wasn't hanging all over him."

"So you recognize her, too, even though she was here only once?"

"Oh, she was here with Larry more than once. As a matter of fact, she used to come in with him two or three times a week. Although come to think of it, I haven't seen her around for about a month or so."

I took the picture back from Ernie and, pointing to Samantha Macabee, said, "This woman was here two or three nights a week with Larry?"

Ernie smiled. "Not her! She came in with Larry only once, about two weeks ago. This was the woman I was talking about." He put his finger on Melissa Randal's face.

I had thought I was ready for Phase Two of the investigation, that part of the job when you take all the information you had collected and started putting the pieces together. Unfortunately, the bartender's identification of Melissa Randal as Goodwin's lady friend and the tapping of my phone threw my plan out of synch. The ride back to Pittsfield gave me plenty of time to arrange my thoughts, however, and I used the time to start plugging this new information into place. It seemed that people were coming in and going out of Larry Goodwin's life, and since timing is everything I concluded that a time frame of Goodwin's history since he had joined Cyber Inc. would be the best way to start putting the pieces of the puzzle together.

Larry Goodwin joined Cyber about ten months ago. There was a definite meeting between him and Melissa Randal about six or seven months ago; the photograph proved that. Was it their first or had they known each other before that? Six months was also how long Goodwin had been placing bets with Lombardi. Up until a month ago Randal and Goodwin had been an item, at least according to Ernie the bartender. Samantha Macabee had put the start of her relationship with Goodwin at the same time he stopped seeing Randal. Was Randal upset at being dumped by Goodwin for Macabee? Was Randal dumped or did she do the dumping? Did she even know about Macabee? Gambling and women, it always seemed to return to those two things.

I made it back to Pittsfield around 9 p.m., shot past the street I lived on and headed to the east side of town to pick up Mario. Curtis Street didn't look any nicer at night than it did during the day, but it did look cleaner. That was because the one street light on Curtis was broken and I couldn't see the trash. I pulled up in front of DeRigger's flat, but before I could get out of my car his front door opened and he waltzed out and over to my car. He opened the passenger door, jumped in, looked at me and said, "Hey, don't you look sharp! Have a hot date?"

"No date, but it was hot," I answered as I pulled away from the curb. "I found some interesting new facts to go with the information I already had."

I filled Mario in on the news that my phone was bugged, mainly because I didn't want him using it while he was at my house working on Goodwin's computer. I didn't see any reason to fill him in on Melissa Randal and Goodwin being an item, especially since he didn't have background on the rest of the case; it would have been meaningless to him, and besides I was planning on keeping that little jewel of knowledge to myself for awhile. We stopped at a pizza place, grabbed two large pies to go and were at my place forty-five minutes after picking up Mario.

I led DeRigger into the house, letting him carry the pizza since I figured he'd eat most of it himself anyway, and got him set up at my computer workstation. He pulled Goodwin's computer out of the box he and Jenny had packed it in earlier that day, hooked it up to my monitor and in moments was ready to go. Mario powered up the machine, then he and I both stared at the monitor screen waiting for the boot up message. In about ten seconds the words "WAS KILLED" flashed on the screen, hung around for another two or three seconds and then vanished.

"Isn't this where I left you this morning?" I asked Mario sarcastically. "Tell me you've gotten somewhere between then and now."

122

"Actually, I have," said DeRigger not bothering to turn in his seat to face me. "I discovered Goodwin's program is definitely not using the computer's internal clock to determine when to advance the message."

"Then how does it know when to change the words?"

"This Goodwin guy was pretty sharp. He included a countdown program along with the message program; from the time a new message begins flashing on boot up, a countdown begins. Basically it becomes meaningless what the internal clock says."

"So," I said, "that means we couldn't have moved the clock up in time to see a new message like we wanted to."

"Correct," agreed Mario. "But in a way, that's good for us."

"How so?"

"Because I now know how Goodwin protected his program. If he's bypassing the clock with his own timer, then that's his safety measure. He probably didn't put any erasure commands in the program, figuring nobody would be able to tamper with it anyway."

"So in effect, you spent the whole day trying to crack the program so now you can tell me the program can't be cracked? Grab your pizza, Mario, I'm taking you home."

"Not so fast, Dunleavy." Mario smirked as he leaned back in his chair. "Goodwin figured he had enough safety to keep all the other honest-to-gosh computer engineers at Cyber from breaking into his program, and he was right. He never counted on a hacker like me being brought in to do the job."

"But you haven't done the job," I groused. "That's the point. Thank God I'm not paying you by the hour because you haven't done much in the six hours or so you had to work on this thing at Cyber."

"I really hate it when people think they know all about computers just because they can turn one on," replied Mario, shaking his head. "Now that I know Goodwin's safety features, I can go about bypassing them without worrying about erasing the whole program."

"Then why didn't you do that this afternoon at Cyber?" I exploded, frustrated at Mario's condescending attitude.

"I was about to do that just before your little call informing me that I was about to return to a life of crime."

"Oh," I mumbled, "well...go ahead then. Don't let me stop you. I'll just go and... grab a piece of pizza."

Which is exactly what I did. Or to be more precise, I had three pieces of pizza, all while Mario went about breaking into Goodwin's code. Just as I was finishing my third piece, it finally came.

"Bingo!" cried Mario.

"You got it?" I said, jumping off the sofa and throwing my crust into the pizza box. I went over to the computer for a better look.

"Of course I got it," he answered. "Unless of course you mean did I get the message program."

"What did you get then?"

"The countdown program. Look! You were right when you said it was changing messages every day."

Mario pointed to the screen, but he might as well have been pointing out the window at the North Star. I couldn't make a thing out of the numbers and symbols that were floating all over the monitor.

"Well," I began, "it's nice to know I was right about something in this case. Now show me where I was right."

"It's here," Mario said, pointing on the screen to the largest group of numbers I had ever seen in one place. "I know you don't understand the concept, so just let me say this number is the computer's way of recognizing twenty-four hours. Notice how the number is changing every second."

"So when is the twenty-four hour period up?"

"In about...three minutes," calculated Mario.

"Oh, that's great! Do you mean to say you and I could have sat here shoving our faces with pizza all this time and we still would have had the final part of the message?"

"Hey, look Dunleavy," started DeRigger, rising from his chair to face me. "You hired me to crack a code created by a computer engineer and I did it in a little over six hours. In my business, that's pretty good. You want something better than that, go hire Houdini!" Mario pushed by me, went over to the table and grabbed a large slice of pizza, flopped onto the sofa and took a big bite.

I hate it when other people are right about me being wrong. Mario deserved an apology from me, and he got one, sort of.

"Okay," I said, "you did just what I asked you to do and you did break the timing code or whatever it is before the message changed. Now what do you say we shut this thing down and re-boot it in three minutes?"

Mario looked up at from the sofa, a big chunk of pizza in his mouth, shrugged and smiled. He rose from the sofa, went over to the computer and shut it down. Neither he nor I said anything for the next few minutes; I was staring at my wristwatch, waiting for it to hit eleven o'clock and Mario was over at the table grabbing another piece of pizza. I went into the kitchen, grabbed a couple of beers from the refrigerator, shook one as hard as I could, then retraced my steps to the computer room. I threw the can I had shaken to Mario, opened mine and took a pull. Mario thanked me, cracked his can open and sputtered when the beer shot all over his face. So much for my having to apologize.

"Sorry," I said over my shoulder as I booted up the computer.

"Right," said Mario, coming over to view the monitor and wiping his face as best he could on his sleeve.

Neither of us said a word as the machine went through its opening series of commands. Suddenly it appeared on the screen, the message we had been waiting for. In large capital letters, the word "BY" booted up, stayed around for a few seconds then disappeared.

Chapter 12

"That's it?" I said, looking from the monitor to Mario and then back again. "That's what we waited all day for?"

"Listen, Dunleavy," said Mario returning to the pizza box for another round. "It's not my fault Goodwin decided his farewell note needed to be grammatically correct." He took a huge chunk out of the piece, chewed and swallowed part of it, then added, "God, I'm hungry."

"Is food all you can think of right now?" I asked. "We have to wait another entire day to get the next message, and even that might not be the last one!"

Mario grabbed his beer off the table, took a long pull and then shoved the rest of the pizza in his mouth.

"Where have you been the last couple of minutes?" he asked smiling, a piece of pepperoni falling from his mouth. "Didn't I tell you I hacked into his countdown program? All I have to do is change the countdown start from twenty-four hours to, say, one minute. That's how long you'll have to wait for the next message."

I stared at Mario, who was taking another drink from the beer can to wash down his food. "So when were you planning on coming over here to set the counter? Next week?"

"I told you I was hungry. Hacking is a lot harder than people think. A man gets an appetite working, you know. Well, actually, you wouldn't know. Private investigators don't really work, do they?"

"No," I answered, "they just pay wise-guy hackers three hundred dollars, but not before all the work gets done. Now ask yourself, what's more important: the money or shoving your face with pizza?"

"Okay, okay," smirked Mario as he made his way to the computer. "Now if you'll just back out of the way, I'll set the timer for one minute and then we'll see the next part of the message."

"We'd better," I snarled as I moved a few feet to my left to let Mario into the seat before the monitor. He quickly got himself back into the countdown program, and after a few quick (so quick it might even have been a few dozen) keystrokes, the program began counting down again. One minute later, after it had reached zero and Mario had restarted the machine, he and I waited impatiently for the new message to appear. It did.

"So who's that?" asked Mario, looking from the name on the monitor back to me. "Somebody you expected?"

"To be honest, I had several names in mind. So while I can't say I expected this one I'm not really too surprised. But I don't think this was a one-person job. Can we run the countdown again and see if another name pops up?"

"Not a problem." He turned back to the monitor, re-entered the countdown program and again set it for one minute. After the countdown and subsequent reboot, a second name appeared.

"Another name I don't know," said Mario. "Are you surprised yet?"

"No," I answered. "This one I expected. And unless I miss my guess, there's one more name on the list. Let's find out."

Mario went through his machinations again and sure enough a third name appeared.

"This name I know," he said.

"I was sure you would. The picture is starting to take shape. I don't think we'll get anymore names appearing, but to be on the safe side let's run the countdown again." Three minutes later a capital letter "I" appeared on the monitor.

"You were right again," said Mario. "We're back at the beginning of the program. So now what?"

"I need to think," I answered, walking over to the pizza box. It was empty, so I threw it aside and grabbed a piece from the second pie. I walked over to the sofa, plopped myself down and took a swig from my beer.

"I like the way you work," smiled Mario. "But if I'm going to sit here watching you eat, drink and vegetate, I might at least look busy." He got to his feet, shut down the computer, detached it from the monitor and returned it to its box. He hooked my computer up to the monitor then turned back to me.

"Where should I put Goodwin's computer?" he asked. "I hope you have a good hiding place around here, because I'm sure you don't want those people whose names popped up a few minutes ago to find out you have it."

I had been deep in thought, so deep I was beginning to get lost. Mario's words, however, brought me back into the light. I stared up at him and then a grin played out on my face.

"As a matter of fact, my friend," I said rising from the sofa, "that's exactly what I want to happen. Come on; let's get another beer. I have to flesh out my plan, and then I have to take you home so you can make a phone call."

Two hour later I was pulling up in front of Mario's house. He got out, holding the pizza box with the last three slices in it.

"Now remember what to do," I said as he shut the door and turned back toward the open car window. "Wait thirty minutes before you call; that should give me enough time to get back home. You know what to say?"

"I'm not an idiot, Dunleavy," replied Mario. "I call you up, tell you that I cracked Goodwin's code late this afternoon while I was at Cyber and that I want you to meet me at my place so I can give you the names."

"Correct. Then I ask why you can't give me the names over the phone, and you answer…"

"That I don't give you the names until you give me the three hundred bucks you agreed to pay me for the hacking job. Speaking of which, Dunleavy, just when do I get the money?"

"As soon as you get hungry again, Mario," I smiled. "It's in the pizza box." Just then I looked in my rear-view mirror and saw two headlights coming up the street. They slowed and the car they were attached to pulled in behind me. In the back glow of the street lamp behind the car I could make out three figures.

"Our friends are here, Mario. Let them in, get settled and then make the phone call."

"All right, Dunleavy," he answered pulling away from my car. He suddenly stopped and stuck his head back through my window. "But I don't really think I like the idea of making myself a target for a measly three hundred dollars. How about if we make it an even…"

"Sorry, Mario," I interrupted, "but three hundred is the going rate for a sitting duck. Now get going!" And with that I pulled away from the curb and began the trip back home. I looked in my mirror as the three men got out of the car that had pulled in behind me and approached Mario. He nodded to them and then led them to his house. I hope he didn't get too friendly with them and offer some of his pizza. Those guys would be just as liable to take the money as the food.

One of my great failings is that I'm not introspective enough (other people might call it being shallow). I don't spend enough time looking deeply into myself, honestly appraising my faults and weaknesses as well as my strengths, and as a result don't bother to see the down side of many of my more ingenious ideas. I get a thought and run with it, always with the belief that it will turn out exactly as I planned. To be perfectly frank, they almost never turn out as planned, but they do always seem to work. The reason I say this now is that after a mere hour of planning, I had devised a scheme that would catch Larry Goodwin's killers, but at the same time put not only my life in danger, but Mario DeRigger's as well. It's the little details I almost never seem to think through.

I arrived home about twenty minutes after dropping off Mario. I could tell you that I simply plopped down in my easy chair and waited patiently for the phone call, but the truth is I was so excited I nearly wore a hole in the rug with my pacing. The minutes wore down much more slowly than they usually do, but the phone did eventually ring. It was Mario and we went through our act, although the little creep mentioned that I had offered him five hundred dollars to hack Goodwin's computer, not three hundred. I made a wish that he would have trouble getting melted cheese off the fifties I had left in the pizza box.

I hung up the phone receiver. As Sherlock Holmes would say, the game was afoot!

I like to think while I drive, and this case was giving me a great opportunity to think. I had spent more time in my car over the past two days than I had in month, but it had been worth it. In retrospect, finding Goodwin's murderers hadn't been that hard. Murderers make more mistakes than, say, bank robbers. Bank robbers plan their crime in a cold unemotional way. But murder is always a crime involving emotions. It could be greed, jealousy, hate or something else, but it is always some emotion. Therefore, murderers always make some emotional mistake; that is, unless you're dealing with cold-blooded professional killers, which I was. But fortunately, I was also dealing with a panicky killer.

If finding the identity of the killers was fairly simple, convincing the other participants in this little drama that I had done so wasn't. I had spent as much time on the phone (my cell phone, since it was the only one I felt safe using) convincing the police to help in the capture as I had devising the plan. Fred Martin was not too happy about my putting myself and another "civilian" in the line of fire, but I finally convinced him that the computer messages naming Goodwin's killers would not be proof enough in court. After all, Goodwin's computerized declaration could have been written by anyone (at least, that's what any competent defense attorney would say). The killers had to be brought out into the open, and the only way to get them to move was to offer the computer to them. Unfortunately, that also meant offering Mario and myself as well.

After making the arrangements with Fred, I hung up and made a second phone call. I have to say that, in all honesty, it was the hardest phone call I have ever had to make.

I arrived at Mario's house fifteen minutes after his "extortion" phone call to me. The car that had pulled in behind me when I had dropped off DeRigger earlier that night was now gone. I wasn't worried, however, because I knew they were just playing it safe and had driven it to a side road so it wouldn't be spotted. I parked in front of the house, got out and walked up to Mario's door. He opened it before I could knock, saying, "I was watching for you and saw you drive up." He said this in a slightly louder voice than normal, making me think he wanted some "unseen" visitor to hear him. I just pushed by him and went inside.

"So you think you've solved the computer program," I said once I was in the living room and he had the door shut. We needed to continue the charade in case the murderers were already in the house. They were.

There was a loud noise in the kitchen, and Mario and I both spun around in time to see Phil Morrissey standing in front of the door leading to the back porch. He was holding a gun and pointing it directly at us.

"Hello, Dunleavy," he said smiling. "You made pretty good time. I just managed to jump over the fence when you drove up. I had been hoping to get in before you showed and grab the computer."

"How do you know about the computer?" I asked, making it sound like I was still in the dark about the tapped phone.

"A little bird told me. Now shut up and give it to me."

I looked at him for a second, mentally calculating the probability of my reaching him in a quick leap. I may have failed math in high school, but even I could figure the odds as pretty long. Morrissey saw my hesitation and the look in my eye.

"Don't even think about it, Dunleavy. You had a reputation when you were on the force for being quick, real quick. But nobody's fast enough to outrun a bullet."

I took a quick glance at Mario, who was slowly sliding sideways. Morrissey saw him as well.

"And you stay right where you are, too," he said to Mario. "Not that a little computer geek twerp like you could cause much trouble." He shook his gun towards me. "Get your bony little ass back next to Dunleavy."

Mario did as he was told. We both knew we had to draw this little scene out a while longer, at least until Morrissey's partner in crime showed, but there was no sense in pushing the danger level any higher than we had to.

"So you killed Goodwin," I said in a conversational tone, or at least as close to conversational as I could come with a gun pointed six feet from my face. "What did you have to do with him?" I knew, of course, but I didn't want him to know I knew.

"Goodwin did a little work for some people I'm associated with," Morrissey answered, slowly advancing into the living room. He was only four feet from me now and the odds were getting better.

"What job? What people?"

"That's none of your business." He looked back at Mario and pointed the gun at him. "Now give me the damn computer, or do I blow your head off and search the house myself?"

It was now or never. Morrissey had approached to within three feet of me as he threatened Mario and, better yet, wasn't pointing his gun in my direction. Do you remember me telling you earlier about the three types of decisions a person has to make in his or her life? On the surface, this appeared to be one of those big life-changing choices. Should I try to jump Morrissey and go for the gun? If it worked I would have the drop on a murderer; if it didn't, I would be laying on the floor in a pool of blood just like Larry Goodwin. And if it was such a huge choice, why did I make my decision the same way I choose what to have for breakfast? No thought, no weighing of options, just go for it.

I went for it, and thank god Morrissey was right about my being fast. I grabbed hold of his gun with my left hand and brought my right fist up to his jaw. Morrissey went down hard, but he left his gun for me to hold. I spun it around in my hand and pointed it down at him, just in case he had any ideas, or ability, to stand up.

"Nice job, Dunleavy," said Mario sidling up to me. "While he was worried about the 'twerp,' you nailed him."

"Yes, quite impressive, Barry," came a voice from the kitchen. "Now drop the gun!"

Mario and I both brought our heads up from looking at Morrissey. Melissa Randal was standing there, a gun of her own pointed at us.

Chapter 13

"I said drop the gun," she repeated. "I would really hate to kill you, at least not just yet."

I threw the gun onto the sofa so a sudden jarring of it wouldn't cause it to fire accidentally. Morrissey slowly got up, rubbing his jaw where I hit him. He looked at me for a second, his eyes blazing. He then went over to the sofa and picked up his gun and slowly walked back toward Mario and I. Just as he reached us, he quickly brought his gun above his head and prepared to bring it down on my face.

"Stop!" ordered Melissa Randal. "It was your own careless fault for losing your gun. You got what you deserved."

Morrissey shot a look at the woman, but as his face was turned away from me I couldn't tell what he was thinking. In any event, after a moment he lowered his arm and backed up a few feet.

"Now you," she said, pointing her weapon at Mario, "will tell us where that computer is or I will have Mr. Morrissey here shoot your kneecap off."

"Officer Morrissey, you mean," I interrupted. "The assistant mayor of Pittsfield and a police officer, the brains behind a murder. Who would have thought it?"

"No one would have thought it, Barry. That's the beauty of the whole thing. No one that is, until you."

"He didn't know," said Morrissey. "He didn't know until you and I showed up tonight. He's not as smart as you think he is, Melissa. Or he thinks he is, for that matter. You've spent the last two days worrying about him for nothing"

"I may not have known for sure, but I did suspect. You're real sloppy, Morrissey. You kept showing up in this investigation in too many places at too many times not to be involved somehow."

"What are you talking about, Dunleavy?" he asked, a sneer on his lips.

"The first time I heard your name in connection with Goodwin's is when I found out you made sure all the cops in town knew about him and a black-haired woman driving around town in a fancy red sports car. That would be, by the way, Samantha Macabee."

"Very good, Barry," smiled Randal. "I see you've done your homework."

"The question is why you wanted people to know," I continued. "The timing of your announcement threw me at first. It was two weeks ago or so, a long time before the murder. Which meant you were planning to kill Goodwin as far back as that. But why? Was it business or a personal matter?"

"What do you mean, 'business' or 'personal'?"

"Well, did you kill him because he dumped you and started going with Macabee? Was it jealousy? Or did you have to kill him because he was getting greedy and wanted a bigger cut of the profits?"

"What profits?" asked Mario, looking over at me with a confused look on his face.

"Once I knew the assistant mayor was involved with a Cyber employee who worked on government contracts," I said to him, "it was a simple step to working out that they were involved in rigging the contracts to go to certain firms. Isn't that right, Melissa?"

"Right as rain, Barry. I have to admit you have that part down perfectly."

"And the profits come from where?" asked Mario.

"Kickbacks from the firms that get the contracts," I answered.

"Wrong!" snorted Morrissey. "We don't need to get kickbacks from the firms. We are the firms. Through a chain of dummy corporations, we own the companies that get the contracts with the state and federal governments."

I looked from Morrissey to Randal. It was bigger than I had thought. Kickbacks would have amounted to thousands, even hundreds of thousands, of dollars. The fact that they owned the companies getting huge government contracts meant we were talking millions!

"That eliminates the jealousy theory then, doesn't it, Melissa?" I said.

"Nothing to be jealous of," she smiled, walking over to Morrissey. She gave him a kiss on the cheek. "There's only one man in my life."

No accounting for taste, I thought, but kept it to myself. Instead I asked, "And you decided you didn't need Goodwin anymore?"

"It was Goodwin who decided he didn't need us," answered Randal. "Or should I say, didn't want us. It seems poor Larry had this disgusting streak of honesty. It finally came to the top and he told us he wanted out."

"Even though he was making enough extra money to get him out of debt with professional gamblers, the gamblers you introduced him to."

"You know, Barry," she said, moving away from Morrissey and further back toward the kitchen. It was obvious she had learned to stay as far away from me as she could, especially after seeing her boyfriend hit the ground hard earlier. "You are starting to impress me more and more. You're right, of course, about the gambling part. That was how we snagged Goodwin in the first place. After I met him at the contract signing at City Hall six months ago I knew he was the perfect person to get our scheme working. So I made it a point of, shall we say, 'getting to know him.'"

"Morrissey here didn't mind?"

"There was nothing to mind, except in Larry's fertile imagination. We started going out, I introduced him to my gambler friends and we let his natural competitive instincts take over. We made sure he lost his bets, of course, and in that way we created what you might call a 'market' for our services. We offered Larry a way to make some extra money to get himself out from under."

"But you continued to make sure he lost."

"Naturally. We needed him to continue to rewrite the contracts in such a way that our firms would have an advantage in the bidding phase of the contract awarding process. But Goodwin was starting to get cold feet. The contract rewrites were taking a long time, in effect messing up Cyber's schedule. He was worried someone at the company was catching on to him."

"That would be Donny Sackett," I said. "He was starting to get on Goodwin's case about how long it was taking to get his work done."

"And poor Larry now had pressure on him from both the gamblers and his company," finished Randal. "Throw into the mix that he started seeing that Macabee woman, and it wasn't long before he decided the only way to get out from under all of it was to stop working with us and come clean. I couldn't let that happen."

"So you set in motion the plan to get rid of Goodwin by sending Morrissey out with the story of Goodwin's black-haired bombshell with the red sports car."

"We were hoping to throw suspicion into Goodwin's personal life and away from his Cyber position when the eventual investigation began."

"But you didn't plan on Goodwin laying the whole scheme out in a computer program."

"We thought we had that little problem solved," nodded the woman. "Phil took over last night in the property room, grabbed the laptop, put it inside his newspaper and went to the men's room with it."

"Isn't it wonderful how they keep making those machines smaller and lighter?" smirked Morrissey.

"I was waiting outside the men's room window," continued Randal, "and Phil just slipped me the laptop. Unfortunately, we were unaware of the second machine at Cyber with Goodwin's program on it."

"You were sloppy," I smiled. "You shouldn't have killed Goodwin until you were sure he had left no clues to your identities."

"I have to admit that we moved a little too fast, but Phil was just itching to off poor Larry, and I don't like saying no to Phil. By the way, have you figured out yet how we did it?"

I was on the spot now. Up to this point, I had been letting the two murderers do most of the talking, filling in the small gaps with some deductive reasoning (the only thing I could use since I was still short on facts). So far I had been mostly correct on my guesses, but now I was being asked to fill in the method of the crime. I took a mental deep breath and plunged ahead.

"I think so. What originally threw me was the fact that the logbook of Cyber had Goodwin signing out on Monday night, but not signing back in on Tuesday. You wanted the police and I to spend time trying to track down where he went during that time. The fact is he never went anywhere: not home, not to Samantha Macabee's, not anywhere. He never left Cyber because he was already dead."

"See, Phil," said Melissa Randal turning to her murderous boyfriend. "Didn't I tell you that Barry's intelligence was going to make him a problem? He's already figured it out."

"A little too late." Morrissey smiled.

"Go ahead, Barry," said Randal. "I want to see if you have all the details worked out."

"The log book from Monday shows a police cruiser showing up at the plant to do the usual quick patrol of the grounds around 10:45," I continued. "That was you, Morrissey. What the book didn't show was that you, Melissa, were hidden somewhere in the patrol car. Back seat?"

"Trunk, actually," she answered.

"Morrissey drove around to the back of the plant, stopped the car and got out. He managed to get inside the main building, probably with a key you had obtained from Goodwin. He found his prey in the snack room. He walked up behind him and killed him." I turned to Morrissey. "I have to say, Phil, that wasn't very sporting of you."

"I'll make it up this time around, Dunleavy," said the policeman. "I'll make sure I look you right in the eye when I kill you."

I ignored the remark and went on. "Then Morrissey came back

downstairs and changed clothes with you, Melissa. Morrissey put on a hat and coat, pulled both as tight around his face as he could so he wouldn't be recognized and drove Goodwin's car toward the exit. You got in the police car, turned on the siren and lights as if you had just gotten a radio call and had to hot tail it to some crime or accident scene. You tailgated Morrissey so the security guard, in order to let you out of the parking lot as fast as he could, would let your partner here out first without much of a check. He just waved him out into the street."

"Excellent, Barry, excellent!" laughed Melissa Randal. "You have it all correct!" Then the smile faded from her lips. "Except for one fact. It wasn't Phil who killed Larry, it was me. And to answer your next question, it was just because I wanted to see if I could actually kill someone. Obviously I could, and do you know what? It was a rush! So much so that I'm looking forward to killing you, just as soon as this little man gives us the computer."

She pointed her gun at Mario and said in a very tight and slow voice, "Now, little man, or so help me I'll just kill you and look for the thing myself. In a tiny apartment like this, it shouldn't take too long."

"About a lifetime I would imagine," came a voice from my right. Out of the door that led to the bedroom came Fred Martin and two other detectives. They had their guns drawn and were pointing them at Morrissey and Randal. "That's about how long you and this pathetic excuse for a cop are going to have in jail to think about this," concluded Fred. "Now drop your weapons and get over against the wall."

"You certainly took your time," I said, reaching down to grab the two murderers' guns from the floor where they had obediently dropped them. "I was afraid you were going to wait until they shot poor Mario. Or worse yet, shot me."

"Hey!" said DeRigger, backing up and letting the other two detectives, Donny Prouett and Pete Jacobs, pass him so they could handcuff Randal and Morrissey. "That's not very funny, Dunleavy."

I noticed that while the detectives were somewhat careful not to hurt the woman, they were in no way gentle with their fellow officer. Fred looked over when Morrissey let out a few grunts, but he didn't say anything. Instead, he turned back to me.

"I thought I should get as much of their confession on tape as I could," said Fred, going over to Mario and motioning him to open his shirt. DeRigger did so, exposing the microphone taped to his chest. Fred reached out and yanked the tape, the microphone coming away with it.

"Ouch! Be careful, will you? After all, I have to be in good shape when I go to court and testify against these two scum."

Fred just smiled and walked back over to me. "Besides," continued my ex-partner, "we would have been in a long time ago if you hadn't kept blabbing on and on with all your theories about this and that."

"Yeah," I said, "but you have to admit all my theories were correct."

"Most of your theories, Barry, most. Not all of them."

"What are you talking about? Which one was wrong?"

"The one where you called Randal and Morrissey the brains of the outfit," answered a new voice, once again coming from the kitchen. Everyone shot around to stare at Vinnie Lombardi and his two goons framed in the doorway to the living room. "If those two had any fewer brains than they do, they couldn't give a pair of slugs a run for their money."

Lombardi, followed by his boys, walked into the living room, always keeping his gun pointed at the three detectives. He flicked his gun hand in the direction of Jacobs and Prouett, which was the signal for his men to approach the two cops and grab their weapons. Meanwhile, Lombardi himself approached Fred and took his revolver.

"Now that we're all nice and comfortable, you," he said pointing to Pete, "can remove those handcuffs from the lady and gentleman." Pete grudgingly did so, receiving a shove from Morrissey when the latter's hands were free.

"Vinnie," gushed Melissa Randal, moving over to the gambler and rubbing her wrists, "I was wondering when you would show up."

"You're lucky I came at all. If I wasn't concerned you would blab to the cops all about me, I would have let you rot in a jail cell for the rest of your life."

A concerned look came over the woman's face. "Vinnie, please. You know Phil and I had to take out Goodwin. He was going to tell the police about us."

"Bull! Goodwin wasn't going to talk, and if you had thought about it for an instant instead of panicking you would have realized that. He wasn't going to confess to rigging Cyber's contracts so he could make money; all he wanted was to get out from behind the eight ball. If you had let me handle him, he'd still be alive to make us more money and I wouldn't be here cleaning up your mess."

"Vinnie, you've got to...."

"Shut up! I'll talk to you later. And just be glad it's me doing the talking and not my boys."

Melissa Randal looked at Vinnie's two goons and turned white. I glanced at Morrissey and noticed he didn't look very happy either.

Lombardi turned back to Fred and I. "I told you we would be meeting up again, Dunleavy. Now what was it you said about revenge the last time we met?"

"I said not even a fat fool like you would try to do anything to three city cops and think about getting away with it."

One of Lombardi's two men left his post guarding Pete and Donny, walked over to me and slammed his right hand into my stomach. I doubled over, all the wind going out of my body.

"You would be absolutely right about that, Dunleavy," said Vinnie, a smile playing out on his rubbery face, "...under normal circumstances. Unfortunately, Melissa and Morrissey have put me in an awkward position. I am already an accomplice to the murder they committed, even though they didn't inform me of it until after the fact. In the eyes of the law, I am just as guilty of poor Goodwin's death as they are. And since all they could do to me for killing you and your friends is give me multiple life sentences in addition to the one I would be serving for Goodwin, I can't see a reason not to kill you all now. But I don't have to worry about that, thanks to Officer Morrissey."

"What are you talking about?" asked Morrissey from his perch along the back wall.

"You're about to make up for all the problems you and Melissa created by killing Goodwin, Phil," answered Lombardi looking over towards the cop. "In a while, the bodies of a private investigator and a former drug addict, along with those of four Pittsfield policemen will be found in this apartment."

"Four policemen?" mumbled Morrissey.

"Unfortunately, evidence will come to light of certain illegal activities concerning drugs and yourself, Phil. DeRigger ends up dead, a bullet from your gun the cause. In the process of committing the drug dealer's murder, you have a shootout with these three detectives and all four of you die as a result."

Vinnie nodded and one of his goons who had been standing next to Morrissey raised his gun and placed the end of the barrel next to the dirty cop's temple. Morrissey's face went ashen as Lombardi's hatchet man took the cop's gun.

"Vinnie, please…" began Randal, her voice pleading. "Phil was just…"

"I told you to shut up, Melissa," interrupted Lombardi. "Just be grateful you're not as 'useful' as Morrissey at this point. You and I will discuss your usefulness later."

"What about me?" I asked Lombardi. "How do I die in this scenario you concocted?"

"In the crossfire," smirked the fat man. "And I think it poetic that the bullet that kills you comes from the gun of your ex-partner, Detective Martin."

Lombardi nodded to his two men, who took the cue and pulled silencers out of the coat pockets. They slowly screwed them onto the guns, and then looked up with smiles on their faces.

"No hard feelings, detective," said Lombardi to Fred.

"The hell there aren't," growled still a new voice, once again coming from the direction of the kitchen. Lombardi and his boys, as well as Melissa Randall and Phil Morrissey, spun around.Standing in the kitchen, his gun drawn, was Chief Sarcovich.

Chapter 14

The next day, in the late afternoon to be exact, I was seated in Jake's Tavern looking out the window at the rain falling down in sheets. The weather had returned to its normal April rendition of alternating rain, sleet and gusts of wind strong enough to knock the apple blossoms off the trees, at least those stupid enough to have popped out earlier in the week. I was holding court, my loyal subjects hanging on every word as I explained how I had brilliantly solved the murder of one Mr. Lawrence Goodwin, Esquire. Okay, so they weren't very loyal, and they were only hanging on to what I was saying in between frequent trips to the bar for refills.

"I can't believe you let Sarcovich take credit for solving Goodwin's murder," said Jenny, sipping her first-ever martini and grimacing. She had let Marcus Thomasson, who was sitting next to her, talk her into trying one and it was obvious from the look on her face how much she regretted her decision.

"I told you," I said, smiling at her discomfort, "it was the only way I could think of to get him to agree to my plan when I called him last night."

"I'm shocked you were even able to get him to accept your phone call," said Fred Martin, sipping his beer.

"He almost didn't," I agreed. "When he finally got on the phone and I was able to get a word in edgewise, it took the better part of fifteen minutes before he would even agree to discuss my plan. It took another ten minutes and the offer of crediting him with cracking the case before he came around."

Fred smiled. "Don't think he didn't notice you making him wait in DeRigger's bathroom for a half-hour while Melissa Randal, Morrissey and Lombardi confessed their guts out. By the way, does Mario ever clean that room?"

"I hope not," I answered. "Besides, Sarcovich got back at me. Did you notice he didn't make his entrance on the scene until after one of Vinnie's goons punched me in the stomach?"

"Just call it taking one for the home team," laughed Fred.

"All right, Barry," piped in Marcus. "Enough of Sarcovich. I can read all about how he single-handedly solved the biggest murder in Berkshire County history tomorrow in the papers. After all, he's spent most of the day giving interviews to the *Guardian*, the North Adams papers and all the television stations. I want you to fill me in on the details."

"Such as?"

"Such as, what first put you onto Melissa Randal? You have to admit there is absolutely nothing in her background to even remotely connect her with anything criminal."

"Wrong, Marcus. There was something in her background, and I found it in North Adams. After I was done 'interviewing' Vinnie Lombardi at his place on Tuesday, I made it a point of visiting with a friend in the North Adams police department. That's when I found out about Vinnie's little scheme of getting the college students there hooked into his gambling operation."

"So?"

"You don't know very much about your assistant mayor, do you?"

"You mean 'former' assistant mayor, Barry, and the answer to that question is not as much as I thought I did."

"While Melissa Randal may have graduated from the University of Massachusetts, she began her college career at the Massachusetts

College of Liberal Arts, which at the time she attended was known as..."

"...North Adams State College," interjected Jenny. "That's my alma mater as well, Marcus."

"And that's where she met Vinnie Lombardi?" asked Marcus.

"Not only met him, but started working for him as it turns out," said Fred. "Ms. Randal is being most co-operative in this investigation, probably in the hope of showing a jury how she was just a young girl hopelessly corrupted by the evil gambler. She told us, in the presence of her attorney, that after she got into debt to him while still a freshman, she would pay off those debts by getting other college students hooked on gambling. That's why it was so easy for her to get Goodwin suckered into Vinnie's scheme; she was an old hand at it, might even say she majored in it at college."

"That will sound very convincing to a jury," I said in between sips of my beer. "Especially after they hear the tape recording of her confessing to getting a rush out of killing Goodwin."

"So the city is going to get a real black eye as a result of one of its leading government figures being not only corrupt, but a murderer as well," sighed Marcus, shaking his head and downing his second martini of the day. He raised his arm to get Alicia's attention from the bar for the third round.

"We're in the same boat," agreed Fred. "Morrissey is not going to make it easy for the rest of the force to get any respect for a long time."

"Speaking of Morrissey," said Jenny, who had downed the rest of her martini just to be done with it and had made the sourest face I had ever seen. "How did you catch on to him being part of the racket?"

"As I told him last night, he kept popping into the picture in too many places at too many times."

I finished the last of my beer just as Alicia was bringing another round of drinks to the table. I grabbed a beer off the tray and noticed Alicia had brought not only a martini for Marcus, but also another one for Jenny. I almost laughed out loud at the look on her face.

"Not only did I learn of his spreading the rumor about Goodwin and Samantha Macabee," I continued, "he was also involved in the stolen laptop at police headquarters."

"Speaking of which," said Marcus, "how did he manage to even know about that so quickly? It wasn't common knowledge around the police station."

"Blame Fred," I said.

"What do mean blame me? I never told anyone about that damn computer!"

"Sure you did. You told Melissa Randal."

"What? I never so much as..."

"Tuesday afternoon, right here in Jake's. Don't you remember? We were talking about the case and you mentioned that you were waiting for Harry Prouty to return from vacation so he could check it out."

"So?"

"Just as soon as you finished talking who came in but Melissa Randal. Or did she 'just come in'? She was probably standing behind us for a long time, listening to you explain all about finding the laptop at Goodwin's and how it had some strange message on it. She figured she needed to get rid of that computer that very night, so she called Morrissey. He was out on patrol, but figured he needed to get into the Property room somehow. I think he tracked down Joe Phillips, the regular Property room cop, and found where he was. Morrissey slipped something into his food or drink and poor Joe was sick the rest of the night. Morrissey then volunteered to turn a second shift when Phillips couldn't make it."

"How do you know all this?" asked Marcus.

"I don't 'know' anything; this is all conjecture, except for the part about Randal showing up here on Tuesday. But it all makes sense, and there are just too many coincidences for that not to be the way it happened. Think about it: Melissa Randal needs to get in to the Property room on Tuesday night and the Property room cop just happens to get sick on Tuesday night. She needs to have her partner, Morrissey, get the job of replacing the Property room cop and Morrissey just happens to be in the squad room ready to volunteer. If the police follow through on my little theory I'll bet they find I'm right."

"Oh, you can bet we'll check on it," said Fred. "And I'll bet you a night out at Jake's you have it wrong."

"You're on," I laughed.

"You haven't finished with Morrissey, yet," said Jenny. "Where else does he come into the story?"

I noticed her martini was still sitting in front of her, untouched. It was probably going to stay that way until Marcus also noticed and grabbed it.

"He shows up once more, this time in the Cyber logbook for Monday night. And while his name doesn't appear in the log, the squad car number that patrols the company lot does. Matching that number with the police record of the car Morrissey was assigned on Monday should be easy."

"You make all this sound too simple," said Marcus, shaking his head. "And in retrospect everything fits. But tell me the truth, Barry— would you have solved this case if Goodwin hadn't left that computer program naming his killers?"

"You know, Marcus," I answered, but not before a long pull on my beer. "Probably not as quickly, but I'd like to think that I would have gotten around to the truth."

"Speaking of computers," said Fred. "What's happening with DeRigger? Now that he's had a taste of good citizenship do you think he'll stay on the straight and narrow?"

"Didn't I tell you? After I filled Mikah Johnston in on the whole story this morning, he was so impressed with Mario's ability at cracking Goodwin's code so quickly that he offered our little ex-con a job at Cyber. Mario starts work on Moday."

"What?" cried Jenny. "DeRigger is working at Cyber? You mean I have to see that little weasel every day?" The look on her face was priceless, but not as much as seeing her grab her second martini and down it in one gulp. She raised her arm and waved at the bar. "Alicia! Give me another!"

"Oh no, you don't!" I said to Jenny, waving off Alicia. I stood up, went around the table and slid her chair out. "You and I have a date for dinner at Mikal's and I don't need to be seen in public escorting a drunk."

"Fine," she said, getting to her feet. "But since you're this big-time successful private investigator now, I'm definitely not going dutch. You're paying."

"Okay," I agreed. Mainly I agreed because at my meeting with Johnston earlier that day, he was so pleased with my keeping Cyber Inc. out of the mess (and placing all of the blame at the doorstep of official Pittsfield) that he gave me a rather nice and rather large bonus. Ms. Jenny St. Pierre was going to get the best dinner of her young life.

We said our goodbyes to Fred and Marcus and were almost at the front door when Sammy Brackens walked in.

"How are you, Lieutenant?" he said. "Sorry to hear the chief beat you to the solution of the murder. But it should put the old boy in a good mood for a few days, and that means a better life for everyone at the station."

Sammy obviously wasn't in the loop when it came to the latest news. However, I was sure Fred would see to it that the truth made its way through the force within the week. But for now, I was more than happy to go along with the lie.

"That's the way it goes, Sammy," I smiled. "Win some, lose some."

Just then the door opened again and in walked C.H. McCarthy, AKA "Charlie" McCarthy, head of Cyber's security force. He must have instantly recognized me because a huge smile began playing out on his face.

"Dunleavy! Well, well. I didn't think our future meeting would be this quick, but here it is."

He started coming up to me, his fists once again opening and closing. Sammy, like I said earlier was a good cop and quick on the uptake, and he noticed what was going on.

"Hey, Lieutenant. Everything okay?"

"Who the hell are you?" growled McCarthy, sizing up Brackens and not seeing much of a threat.

"He's a cop," I said. "He's off-duty, though. As are," and here I turned toward the bar, raised my arm to point and said, "him and him and him and him and him. But since they're all off-duty, I'm sure they won't mind if we have our little discussion."

"Uh, Lieutenant," began Sammy, "I don't think that's such a good…"

"Hey, kid! Kid! You, Brackens!" It was Fred calling, still seated at our table with Marcus. "Get over here! I want to talk to you!"

Sammy looked from Fred to me, and then back to Fred. Since Fred was his superior on the force, he had no choice but to amble over to the table. Fred pushed out the chair I had been sitting in and motioned the young cop to have a seat. Sammy sat.

"What are doing interfering in Barry's business, kid?"

"But sir," stammered the younger cop, "it looks like they're about to, about to…"

"Have a discussion," Fred finished the sentence.

"Yes, sir. But that other man is so much bigger than the lieutenant, I just thought…"

"The day Barry Dunleavy can't handle that tub of lard is the day I'll buy you a drink. But that day isn't today, so you can buy me a drink."

Sammy looked at Fred for a long moment, looked up at me (I was still holding my ground and smiling), then back to Fred. He then duly nodded his head and started to get up, but my ex-partner grabbed his shoulder and pushed him back into his chair.

"Better yet, let's have the mayor here buy us both a drink. What do you say, Marcus?"

"My pleasure, gentlemen. Say, son, you don't happen to drink martinis, do you? No? That's okay. Alicia! Two beers and another martini!"

"Now that that's settled," I said, looking away from the mayor's table and back toward McCarthy, "we can get on with our business. But not here."

"Where?" he asked.

"Out back by the dumpster. I don't want the busboy to have to haul your heavy butt far to dump the garbage."

"You're going to regret you ever met me, Dunleavy," he said and walked past me and towards the back door.

"Barry?" whispered Jenny.

"It's all right, honey. You go out to the car and get it started. I'll be there in just a minute."

She looked at me for a moment, then slowly made her way to the front door and went outside. I turned and followed McCarthy's path out the back way.

Five minutes later, the busboy wheeled a large garbage can from the kitchen through the back door, saw me standing there and began making his way to the dumpster.

"Hello, Mr. Dunleavy?" he asked. "Could you give me a hand with that dumpster lid?"

"Sure, Jimmy," I answered. I turned to the dumpster and lifted the top. Inside was Charlie McCarthy, blood trailing from his mouth and a dull, glassed-over look in his eyes. He was vainly trying to say something, but no sound made its way past his moving lips.

The busboy frowned, looked at the man lying in the refuse, then shrugged and tossed the contents of the can he had wheeled out of the tavern into the dumpster. I let the lid of the dumpster drop with a loud bang.

Five minutes later Jenny and I were halfway to Mikal's.

The End